UNDER THE WITCH'S CAP

A FINE COLLECTION OF SINS BOOK 1

GŌSHEN HEXX

VICTORY WOMAN PRESS

The Lineage of Albert Whitmore

1860-1966-Albert Whitmore (d. 1966 at 106 years of lung cancer and dementia)-Albert Sr.

1872-1886-San Lin Cho (d. 1886 by drowning/murder)

Children of Albert & San Lin:
1880-girl (deceased)
1882-boy (Lem Albert Whitmore) Albert Jr. d. 1977 electrocution
1883-boy (Lee Albert Whitmore) Albert 1st
1884-girl (deceased)
1886-unknown sex of child at San Lin's death
Lem Albert and wife
3 boys born, 1902, 1904, 1906. All named Albert.
Alberts 2nd, 3rd, 4th, 5th

Lee Albert and wife
4 boys born, 1904, 1905, 1908, 1911. All named a variation of Albert. All deceased young.
First son of Lem Albert and wife
1930-boy named Albert-Albert the 6th
Albert the 6th (son of Lem), and wife from Hong Kong
1970, girl. Named Alberga.
Alberts by Lee
No wives reported. Worked as fortune tellers from 1930-1975.

Alberga and Alberto Sanchez
One daughter, Alberta Sanchez, born 2006

AUTHOR NOTE

In the mid-1930s my grandfather, a worker in the coal mines under Bellingham, Washington, brought home a small human skull, saying to my grandmother in front of my mother and her two sisters that it was the skull of "one of them Chinese child workers who drowned in the mines."

The mine collapse and deaths are historical facts. Local legends.

My grandmother made my grandfather bury the skull in a wooded area now known as Toledo Hill in south Bellingham.

In the late 1999 through 2023, I was the school secretary for a middle school built smack-dab atop Bellingham Coal Mine Number One. When I was a teenager one could enter Bellingham Coal Mine Number One about twelve feet before the concrete and wooden barrier blocking it stopped the progress. Sinkholes opened in the neighborhood and one parking lot was riddled with buckled concrete due to subluxation.

The access tunnels under the school would flood and the custodian found all kinds of oddities. A lawn chair. A bisque doll's head. A gold ring. He gave me the ring and told me to write a story about it. I have that ring and it is next to my computer as I write this tale.

The school was torn down, and the mine tunnels backfilled. I peered into them before their end and, that day began writing "A Fine Collection of Sins." My father was a part-time antique dealer, and I have artifacts and documentation from his collection regarding Bellingham Coal Mine Number One.

This novel is in tribute to the children who lost their lives therein.

PROLOGUE

I t no longer mattered that she had been able to loosen the bindings fixing her ankles to the iron eyebolt drilled into the floor of the shaft. The water now touched her chin. Inky black coal-infused liquid death. Oddly—or perhaps not so odd in that one's life is often said to pass before one's eyes at death, she thought of her grandmother's calligraphy lesson using black pigment. *Black encompasses all colors. They swirl and mix. They marry and beget something new. Something so deep that all things are contained within it. Black is not to be feared. It incorporates all which exists in one smooth, rich hue. It is the spectrum of life.*

Soon, I shall drown in its gloriousness. My lungs shall fill and this life...this incarnation, will end. The life inside me, will end. The scent of death lingered about her. Three smaller children had already drowned, their faces turned inward into the darkness. Their lives had been hers to protect and her own arrogance had seen to their demise. *Had I obeyed, they may have all lived to see another day. Perhaps lives without being enslaved. I am a fool. They would have been enslaved. Why fool myself with hopeful daydreams in the last moments of my life?*

Whether she ironed shirts or suffered indecent liberties, she had been *his* slave. She had not been born into that hell—but the children she had birthed—they were slaves. A pitiable existence. Perhaps death by black water was preferable.

What kind of life would they have led—the children now lifeless before her? If they survived their first hours of life, they became playthings of the loathsome and perverse polite ruling class of Beacon Shores. Truly, these gentlemen, were the *bak gwai*--white devils--of whom her grandmother had warned. They offered work and marriage. Prospects above one's station. And worse, they offered hope. Then took it away. Children born of that hope were offered nothing. That was the cruelest blow. It was the true meaning of hell. To strip one of hope.

She had made the trip across the Pacific with a dozen others. Her parents believed the lies of the affluent American Albert Whitmore.. He owned a town on the opposite coast in America. He was certain the territory he was developing would become a state. He gave them money. Not Yuan. British pounds. Worth its weight in gold. He bought her, her sisters, her cousins. Some boys. Some girls. All between the ages of seven and fourteen. Grandmother did not approve of such things. Who could give a girl a better life than her own people?

Grandmother had shared many lessons covering the aspects of life and death. It was the way of her clan. The village shaman, Grandmother held sway and power. And her lessons were served like tea across a table. San Lin knew, by rote and recitation, what was expected of her at this final moment. Water teased her nostrils. Death kissed her with each inhalation—little desperate struggles for air.

Each aspect of demise had an intonation. A gesture. Death was as much a dance as life. How one danced with death was as important as how one danced in life. To the granddaughter of a shaman, the rituals of death were expected to be honored. The ancestors were always watching. They would judge her and the manner in which she met and embraced darkness.

There were many ways to die. Death at the hands of another. Death by illness. Death by one's own hand. Death by the hooves of horses. Death by beheading. She had expected death by natural causes. Old age. The inevitable ravages of time. Not this. Not death by drowning in a land far from the bones of her ancestors, her body split and broken and filled with the growing seed of her abuser. She knew she was not the first Chinese worker to die at the hands of a cruel taskmaster, nor would she be the last. Chinese labor was plentiful and cheap. She was just one of many to meet an end in the mines of Beacon Shores, Washington Territory, in the English year 1886.

The traditions of her people said her ancestors would help her avenge death by murder--if given a name with which to cling when the decedent crossed over the mountains of death. She would give the name voice and carry just enough of it in her final breath to exact revenge. It made her feel ugly—the desire to see her killer stripped of dignity, livelihood, society, family and flesh. What was done to her was a thing no human should do to another. To repeat her anguish against him—was that more debt for her soul to carry or would it bring a measure of freedom and satisfaction? And how long would it take?

She had sons. Sons who would carry her blood into future generations. Sons she had barely seen before they were secreted away like dirt under a rug. Her first son came the winter of 1883. The next, but eleven months later. Then, there were two girls. One of whom was born with bright blue eyes and reddish hair and thereby was saved from immediate termination of life in the mines. Though she has now breathed her last in this flooded shaft but feet from where San Lin now struggled to capture one final breath. Even English features could not save her. The other daughter went to the mines before she had tasted her mother's milk. And now, there was another life growing in her belly. One that would end. *I am barely eighteen years old and have successfully ushered four children into this world. Two survive. My sons live. Males have privilege in Beacon Shores, just as in China.*

She inhaled deeply and held her breath. She then slowly exhaled the name of her killer. The boss man who had used her body for his vile pleasures and slave labor. The boss man who had forced her to watch her own child die. *Ancestors! Hear me now! As I leave this life I want you to know of his crimes against our family. He is evil! He called me wife and forced a gold band upon my hand. He forced me to attend his church. He gave me children, then stripped them from my arms. Watch over my sons, for they live...somewhere. My daughters are dead. One died in the mines. Foully used to predict poisonous gas. And why use the girl babies? Because the little yellow birds are too expensive to raise or have shipped in. The boss can make many babies and it doesn't cost him a thing.* His name sickened her--the owner of the mine in which she would now meet death. She breathed it out harshly. "Albert Whitmore." She held the final syllable of his name on her lips as the water rose above her chin. Her last words would be the name her ancestors would harbor and protect until vengeance could be met.

Her belly fluttered. Her child kicked. This little one, through no fault of its own, would never see the light of day, and alas, would have only the evil name of its father to carry it through the darkness. She did not feel love for the baby. She pitied it. It was the product of violence. It was shameful to her that she had not killed herself after the first time he took her. That is how things were handled in the old country, where her grandmother's spirit waited for her to make offerings at the altar of the ancestors. It was an old tradition of her people, but one to which she had been taught to cling. *Death before defilement. Death before enslavement.* Even as she had crossed the Pacific under the promise of work and freedom— these things were sacred to her.

There had been chances during her short life in America to meet death honorably before her lungs filled and eyes grew dim in the blackness of the mine shaft. She had not been able to throw herself from the highest window to save herself. She had not the courage to plunge a kitchen knife into her own belly. Did she dishonor her ancestors by continuing to breathe and suffer the abuses of her captor? It had been her constant thought. *Death before defilement.* Thoughts tormented her. It was through no fault of her own that she had been abused. *I am innocent. But I am defiled. Perhaps death is a blessing, after all.*

San Lin welcomed the tingling numbness. She had long lost sensation in her legs from the chill. Now, every part of her body, inside and out, met icy death. With his name on the tip of her tongue.

Somewhere, far away, her ancestors stirred.

CHAPTER ONE

Sanz wandered the length of the town three times before stopping at the edge of the pier to express, quite vehemently, and quite loudly, that which she had allowed to go unsaid since the move.

"I am in Hell."

And Hell has a blue sky, calm waters, a well-maintained boardwalk and pier, and it's got to be a trick.

She startled as her proclamation met with a reply. "Beacon isn't Hell. At least not in the traditional fashion. I've always considered it a branch off the main road to the underworld where one can get good ice cream and decent WIFI, which is free thanks to our progressive mayor. Other than that, yes. It's pretty bleak here."

"I'm sorry. I wasn't aware I had an audience in my pit of despair. The secret is out. There is nothing to do here. Nothing." She walked to the edge of the pier and jumped off to speak to the interloper. He was dressed in a *utilikilt* and old, faded metal band t-shirt. His black hair was tipped hot pink and his blue eyes were rimmed with black liner. He wore fluorescent orange nail polish. And he had guns bigger 'round that she could circle with her thumbs and pointer fingers of both hands together. Muscles. Dude had muscles. And he wore a sporran.

"Hi. I'm Baker. And yes, that is my legal first name. I am Baker Koma Kulshan White. My name is an homage to yonder mountain and my parents' love for all things cold, wet, and icy. Mt. Baker is also known as Koma Kulshan, or the *great white watcher*. I am forever branded a child of Anglo snowbirds. You're the new girl on the hill, huh? The Whittie House."

Sanz smiled inwardly. "Yes. Yes, I am. I'm Sanz."

"You don't leap like a girl. You're a runner? Hurdles? High jump?"

Sanz laughed. "State long jump champion senior year. In Oregon. That's where we're from. Mom and me. And I wasn't aware that jumping off a pier onto the shore was a gender-based activity. You're wearing a conglomerate of styles and have a pink coiffure. Androgynous much? Thou shalt not judge on appearances. I am athletic. And you are..."

"I am...working on intention vs impact when it comes to labels. Welcome to Hell, more properly known as Beacon Shores, Washington. Named for that crumbling lighthouse up the beach, we are the bright beacon of hope for ghost ships passing through the straight in the dead of night. And numerous vessels of better fortune a hundred years ago."

"Coal exports."

Baker nodded. "And you live at the heart of it all. Whittie Manor. Once home to the nefarious Albert Whitmore, a man of incredible wealth and questionable tastes —or so rumor has it."

"Mother and I are his last surviving heirs. He waited for everyone but us to die. A fifty-five-year moratorium on inheritance of the estate."

"That make you rich?"

"No. That makes us up to our asses in dust and of all things, little dishes of salt. I mean, they are everywhere. Tin foil ashtrays filled with salt. Dude had issues."

"Took you all long enough to move in."

"Albie's last will and testament specified that none should inherit his land and properties for fifty-five years after his passing. He was one hundred and six years old at his death and at the time had sixteen living relatives. There are now two. Mom and me." Sanz began the long walk up the beach to the road. "We have inherited the world's mustiest collection of sins, ever."

Baker laughed. "Collection of sins?"

"The house—especially the library, is filled with oddities from all over the world. And then there are the books. Scintillating fore-edge books no doubt tipped with real gold leaf. Japanese pillow books. Fancy French post-cards. And hundreds of old lewd photographs of Chinese mine workers of questionable age. I haven't even fully explored the attic, basement or sub-basement yet. Albert Whitmore was an eccentric, perverted, pedophiliac, egotistical slave owner. And Mommy and I are keepers of his estate and oddities."

"The sub-basement. You don't want to go down there," Baker replied.

"Why not? What do you know? Is this where you tell me of the legend or curse on the house which has been kept secret from the kinfolk for half a century?"

"Well. Yes. Everyone knows the sub-basement leads to a mine elevator and that you can only go down twenty-three feet before you hit a concrete and reinforced steel rebar cap. Old man Whittie had it built to keep the Chinese mineworker's spirits...*below*. There was an accident. Some of the kids died. Drowned. It was after that the old man went kind of nut. He lived most of his life in a downward mental spiral. Had he not been wealthy he would have surely ended up at Western State Mental Hospital. And back then, it wasn't a kind place. It was all iron head cages and straightjackets."

"I know that story. It was one of the more delightful topics of conversation at dinner with the *hellatives* at the Chinese New Year. My mother is great great great grand-daughter of old Albie. Seems he was a bit of a perv and had himself a young Chinese bride from amongst the mineworkers. She gave him children. He sent the male babies away to be raised in another state, under assumed names. There's no record of any girls being born. I'm sure he rolled over in his grave when the estate finally caught up to us. DNA proof positive. It's all ours. And let me tell you—there isn't much. A house we can't touch, art that can't be sold and of course, the ghost. Haven't seen her yet, but we've heard her. Or what we think must be her. What really gets me is that I have an olive complexion, reddish hair and black eyes in a family tree of mostly Chinese Americans. I am a heady mix of Asian, Latin American, and good old European bloodlines. My DNA report is insane. Mother is mostly Chinese. Father was Latino. So if Albie the First was a racist, as I suspect, his decedents are like Heinz 57. Bottle us up and sell us in sixpacks at a warehouse store.."

Baker chuckled. "You're funny. We speak of the ghost

sometimes. Especially when there's been a sighting. We all grew up hearing her tale—she's kind of the local ghost-wandering-the-shore. Sometimes the story adds that she was pregnant when she died."

"My great-great-great-great grandmother was Albert's child bride, San Lin. Granny to the fourth degree died in the mining accident of 1886. She left two children behind, Lee Albert Whitmore and Lem Albert Whitmore, born but a short 11 months after Lee, and was pregnant at the time of her death. My bloodline is screwed, but I don't want to think about that, you know? Baker—I think you and I need to head up to the house, pop open a couple of cold ones, and talk local legends. I have just given you all that I know. You can fill in the details with fact or fiction. I don't care. Since I have now walked the length and breadth of Beacon Shores and shall expire from the intense nothingness of this town...talk to me."

Baker depressed the side button on his phone to illuminate the clock feature. "Yeah. Sure. It's early. It's not like I have to be home at a certain time on a Saturday. Until school resumes after break. The parents ask that I keep regular hours even though I'll be nineteen next week."

"My evil plan unfolds. Let's go. You don't have any gum in your sporran, do you?"

"Yes, I do. And my tarot cards."

"Oh, I am so getting a reading today. Are you attending that highfalutin' community college one town over? I'm enrolled. Start after break. I'm eighteen."

"Yes. I'm a student there. If you need a ride, I own a vintage truck. There's also a bus."

Sanz smiled. *He's cute. If I weren't so dead inside I'd hit on him.* "Thanks."

———

Baker watched his new friend's gait as they walked up the hill to the old house that literally wrote the book on haunted house on the hill. The Whittie Estate. The Manor. The House. The Tomb. The entrance to hell. It had sat empty for over fifty years yet was far from a state of disarray. Groundskeepers tended it. A cleaning crew visited monthly. A light always shown in the upper window of the witch's hat—the peaked and bewitching roof on the side towers of the mansion house. Sanz had a strong pace. He fought to keep up.

The house had a grand total of seventy-two steps from the driveway to the front porch. He'd walked the steps on a dare before. Every kid worth his salt had gone up the old iron and concrete staircase and jogged three times 'round the wraparound porch after dark on a school night. There was an offshoot of the main driveway that led to the two-story glass conservatory—but no one used it. So far.

"This place should be in pretty good shape what with the groundskeepers and cleaning crew."

"Mother fired them. She's so rude sometimes. She's determined to do it all herself. The edges of the bookshelves are clean. The tops of the books look like a feather bed made of cobwebs. The handrail is clean, but the slots in-between the spindles are gross. The dust is so old it is grimy."

"Big place to keep clean for fifty years. They kept the pipes from freezing and the lawn trimmed. New paint and glass replaced when needed. Except in the greenhouse."

"You must know the caretakers."

"Local business."

"Well, maybe after Mother doesn't have steam piping from her ears and the cry of a dying banshee as a voice, she'll look into hiring them again. She's pretty obsessed right now with putting things in order. She quit her job in Portland to move here. She's not certain the job prospects are viable in Beacon Shores. The estate has hoops through which she must leap before collecting a dime other than a monthly stipend—which is enough to keep us in Netflix and laundry soap."

"What did she do?"

"Mom is an undertaker. Embalming. Cremation. Your standard burial styles."

"The nearest funeral home is thirty miles inland. There might be a market for cremation services here. As you've noticed, we have one grocery store, one convenience store, a Chinese restaurant, a pizza joint and a handful of other businesses who rely on the ferry service and tourist season."

"Well, as soon as her head is back on her shoulders, I'm sure she'll look into it. We get a stipend from the estate right now. It's not much but keeps us in store-brand soda and Mother's secret vice of nips of brandy." Sanz stopped on step number fifty. "I get winded right about here. One would think an eighteen-year-old athlete would have more stamina. What happens during the tourist season?"

Baker laughed. "I know my limits. I was done around the fortieth but pushed on so that I didn't look weak. And tourist season brings drones and lookie-loos to this monstrosity on the hill. And foot traffic for the ferry. Just wait until the drones start passing overhead. Townies are already freaked out that you've moved in—

and tourists have been dying for the ghost tour for decades."

"I would have never thought you were weak. Kind of an odd thing of a gay guy to say about himself."

Baker coughed. "Not gay. I am gender nonconforming. I aim to be gender neutral, but people have a hard time with that. So, you may address me as a male. You can use he/him/his or if you feel so compelled, they/theirs. I honestly don't care. I am who I am. I wear eyeliner and nail polish and have been known to don a dress from time to time. I am also a state-level youth body building champion. Got me a scholarship to any four-year university I want. But I had this gut feeling I needed to stay near home for now. So...I have strength, but little stamina, you know? For me, who I am is a non-issue. Wearing fuchsia lipstick doesn't make me any more female or any less male. I simply am a citizen of Beacon Shores.

"I love the smell of the twenty-first century in the morning."

"The horrors of Beacon's past kind of keeps us all humble and accepting. Anything short of child labor, pedophilia, forced marriage and murder is no big deal here. This community may have little to offer its youth by way of recreational activities, but at least it is a rather inclusive, accepting place. Unless you are shipping in slave labor—then things get a little iffy."

"Have a boyfriend? Girlfriend?"

"No. You?"

Sanz laughed. "I'm not ready for anything like that. It's enough for me to deal with myself. I am neuro-spicy and have synesthesia, a fabulous IQ, and an eidetic memory, but have a wee bit of difficulty with stress and anxiety. Peopling is hard for me. I've dated. Went to the senior prom in Oregon, but so far, no one special."

"And still you are so well adjusted."

"I don't know about that. I'm not sure anyone who has a blood-tie to Old Man Whittie or this town's past can consider themselves well adjusted."

Baker sniggered. "Yes, well, we are all normal enough being born and/or raised in Beacon—the town built on the backs of Chinese children—sometimes literally—can be."

"Well, when you put it that way, I'm pretty screwed, huh?"

"You and me, both. This town is the bright center of acceptance in a world otherwise, at best, inclusive and at worst, murderous. Love those odds. I'm sure I shall graduate with my AA, attend whichever university gives me the best deal, become an Olympian, then get a job doing something safe, marry and adopt from Nigeria or Laos. And then never move more than five miles from Beacon."

"Tell me about our school, friend."

Baker laughed. "Do you know it's built over one of old man Whittie's mines? Mine Number One. The manor house sits atop number four. Every now and then a sink hole opens in town. The tide still ebbs and flows in the tunnels. Everything is built over the old mines. Still, there is a garden from which we all eat, a LGBTQ club, and an old-fashioned juke box in the commons. There is also an active branch of the Young Republicans and Flat Earth Society. I think those two groups meet in the same room at the same time."

"Troglodytes," Sanz replied. She reached the porch and collapsed into an Adirondack-style chair. "After spring break, I have an appointment with the administration for an entry plan. There must be some concern that I'm as crazy as Whitmore. Or they are in a frenzy because I have an IQ as high as Einstein's, am heir to the local despot's fortune, and am a special needs student, who instead of politely opting to attend school online, has chosen to attend the local community college like a common peasant." She paused. "I'm already bored here. Ready to leave this fabulous porch and enter the inner sanctum of old man Whittie?"

Baker opened the intricately carved screen door. "You don't seem like you're special ed."

"We are just like everyone else, brother. Only sometimes way smarter."

"Well, then, allow me to escort you into the manor house. After you." He wiggled the screen door back and forth.

She stepped through the open door with a pretentious air that made Baker giggle. "Mom?" Sanz called. "Mother!"

"I'm busy!" came a reply from somewhere deep into the darkest recesses of the house.

"Well, I guess Mom won't be serving us Kool-Aid and cookies."

"I will never drink the Kool-Aid—if you get my meaning."

"I get the historical context of Kool-Aid, Baker. Jamestown Massacre of November 18, 1978. Eidetic memory. But it was actually Flavor Aid. Tour? This, as you can see, is the grand foyer, complete with Saint Helena olive wood trim, a tree which is now extinct in the world. You will note the floral inlay on the stairwell. That's African ivory and gold."

"Ivory? Disgusting," Baker whispered.

"Yes, well. True that. But this house is a conservatory of rare things like extinct woods, animal parts, gems, and minerals. The lawyers say we can't change a damned thing. I told Mother I was going to knit a banister cozy to hide the ivory. It makes me sad. Though, some of the old wood is pretty cool. Considering this house was built in 1880 things have stayed fairly well preserved. No doubt some of the soldiers home from the War of Northern Aggression helped build this place."

"Interesting way to describe the Civil War. That's confederate speak."

"My family was Union all the way so far as I know. The phrase is from the spine of one of the books I dusted. Haven't read it yet." She paused. "This place was built by employees of the Albert Whitmore Company. So...this... this vaulted monstrosity is the grand foyer, as I said. Nifty, huh? That's silk wallpaper and a hand-painted fresco on the ceiling. I can smell it. That's part of the synesthesia. Cherubs smell like soot." She paused thoughtfully. "I haven't quite figured out what it depicts yet. I'm sure it's Pre-Raphaelite sexual symbolism with all those naked cupids and bosomy women. I am eternally grateful it appears to lack the face of Old Albie superimposed upon one of the cherubs. The staircase to the right leads to the east wing—which is closed off. The stuff up there is all covered with tarps and Mom just stands at the top and sighs when she looks at it. Big job. And neither one of us can get past the toybox with the scary clowns painted on it. Creepy. Staircase on the left leads to the rooms we are using presently. The upstairs bath is a religious experience. And I mean that literally. The sink is mounted on an old pulpit—right out of *Moby Dick*. The non-descript door that blends into the paneling just ahead of us leads to what must have been the servant's quarters and places below. Not even a doorknob. Just a press of the hand and it opens. And places below...well... uncharted territory. The attic can be reached from either wing. The room in the witch's cap can be reached only by one hell of a narrow climb, is locked and we don't have the key. Not sure how that light goes on at dusk and off at dawn. We assume it is on a timer. Oh, and I found this in the sub-basement."

Sanz held her right hand to display a gold wedding band.

"I'm keeping it. There's something about this ring that brings me comfort in an otherwise troubling situation. Now...that door is something else. We can't just kick open the door or take it off its hinges. The wall and door are carved out of English oak and has strakes of Bornean ironwood. Yes, *strakes* like from an old sailing ship. Albie commissioned the ship to circumnavigate the globe for his priceless woods and *objets d'art*, then had it dismantled. Parts of it were built into this ostentatious house— as evidenced by the bow of the boat sticking out the west wing—which I am certain has been the subject of many drive-by photographs and satellite images. I am surprised you have not yet mentioned that my house has a prow stuck out its side. Suffice it to say, the door to the turret is impenetrable. The lock, we thought, was made of brass. It's not. It's brass and gold. It is fused onto the door with Damascus steel and has Chinese characters carved into it. Some presumed magic spell to keep the kids he was abusing under his thumb, maybe. Albie's attorney said the lock was worth about a hundred grand alone in current era dollars. And that law firm is just chomping at the bit for us to mess with stuff. One faux pas and we lose money in the stipend. The locksmith will be here on Monday. If he can't pick the damned thing without marking it up, we're going to leave it closed off until we find the key.

"I plan on making the tower my room—small-ass staircase or not. I always wanted to live in a turret. I belong under a witch's cap." She paused, making a heavy sigh for dramatic effect. "Kitchens—yes, plural—there are two kitchens down the hall to the right. The small kitchen connects to the scullery where I'm sure the servants ate and did what domestics did back in the day. Mom and I actually prefer using that area, as it reminds us of apartment living before we inherited this grand beast of a house. The pantry is larger than my childhood bedroom. Both panties, I should say. There's an entire storage area for salt." She paused. "Don't ask. I will explain. I've had this tour in my head for days. Let me get it out."

"No questions. Carry on," Baker replied.

"I'm not even sure how to describe the main kitchen. It is huge and we have not yet even begun to open all the drawers and cubbies. Upstairs, adjoining the unused east wing, there is the perfunctory grand ballroom which could double as a basketball court if hoops were installed, and below that, a glass enclosed conservatory full of empty planters with an adjoining ladies sitting room furnished with plastic-draped but resplendent green velvet chaise lounges, no doubt to help swooning women gain composure. There is a men's study that is permeated with the odor of pipe tobacco and cigar smoke and scatter rugs dotted with what could only be the stains of spilled brandy and the tears of the oppressed. You can't get to it except through a secret entrance. It is both twisted and bizarre. We know something is *off* about the room—emphasis on the word *off*, mind you, but haven't investigated it too thoroughly yet. We are going to place an ionizer in there to see if we can lift old man smell. Did you know rich old men leave a stink? We may smudge and have the room blessed, too. I swear, the aura is downright unpleasant in there. If it becomes too great to bear, we can just pray away the sins of the past in the chapel."

"There is a chapel? Wow."

"A proper chapel with kneeling benches and gilt icons. And get this...the crucifix is in the shape of a light-house, but Christ is notably absent, for there are impressions where His image must have once been. The chapel is accessed by a door under the stairway to the west wing. There is an altar stone and a cupboard full of stoles and other religious accoutrements. Sweet candlesticks. And of course, pews constructed from rare and/or extinct wood with inlay of dubious origin."

Baker chuckled. "Did this place come with a glossary of terms?"

"More or less, yes. All the exotic woods and inlays and antique Etruscan tiles are cataloged. Most of the furnishings, from knickknacks to antique flour crocks, are listed as well. I read the pdf on the drive up here. Like I said, Albie had issues. Serious issues. He catalogued his workers, too. Sick old fart."

"Where's the library? That's the part that looks like the prow of a ship from the outside, right?"

"To our left, through the walnut veneer pocket doors—the veneer which covers steel, mind you—is his version of a panic room. It doubles as the library and collection room. Truly forefather of all secure areas. As far as I can tell, once inside, there is no exit save for the steel doors. I haven't found a secret passage yet. The library takes up the entire lower west wing of the house, minus the chapel, which shares a wall. There are literally a hundred dishes of salt in there, too. I am systematically vacuuming up the layers of dust atop the books. That, but not the salt. I have to change those and dispose of the "used salt" in the designated salt ditch. I haven't completed the task and Mom's been on my case about it. She walks around the mansion mumbling about replacing the salt...replacing the salt. In English, Mandarin, and Spanish. She's losing it, man. Seriously, the sky will fall if we permanently remove the salt from this house."

"We live in the Pacific Northwest. The sky falls here all the time. It's called rain."

"You're a helpful sort. Shall we?" Sanz used both hands to grasp the heavy iron door pull and pushed. "The doors to Goliath are heavier than sin."

"I've never been in an actual panic room."

"I haven't had a chance to explore every nook and cranny of old Goliath. I'm sure its true purpose is as nefarious as the smoking room upstairs."

"I'm becoming aware that you call the library Goliath."

"After one of the specimens, yes. Old Albie had a flare for decorating, as you will see."

Baker recognized immediately that the room was, indeed, in the shape of a great ship's bow. Porthole windows on the far side and fine brass fittings that could rival those of the Titanic or Queen Mary. Interspersed among the panels of floor to ceiling bookshelves were glass cases, neatly lit from underneath and polished to a high gloss. "Where does one start?" he asked. "I just need to take all this in. I feel like I'm in the library from *Beauty and the Beast*. Did he read all these? Which book is the oldest? How could a man who loves books as much as he obviously did be such a misogynistic pig?"

"One question at a time. Maybe you better sit down. You looked flushed. Truly, you are not the first person to quiver and drool when first setting foot in this *magnífica biblioteca*. If history judged Albert by his collections, they'd think him a great and knowledgeable man. Let's run some numbers, all right?"

Baker nodded. "Freaking impressive."

"There are about fifty-thousand books lining these walls. Not a one of them is younger than sixty years. The oldest is a fourteenth century illuminated manuscript, kept under glass. Albert kept rare art, too. Icons from Greece, sacred texts from India and China and the Egyptian stuff is off the hook. Therein, mind you, is why I refer to the library as 'Goliath.' Tucked away in that large rolltop desk over yonder is a funereal mask from the land of the pharaohs. Small, ornate, gold-gilt and jewel encrusted—it is shaped like a scarab. The accompanying literature says it was created as a death mask for a child whose daddy was a high mucky muck in the whole building-of-the-pyramid-of-Cheops thang. It reminds me of a Goliath beetle."

"That is both perverse and sad. And insanely cool."

"Mom thinks the mask is creepy and says it will be the first thing donated to the Museum of Cairo once we can move the merch freely. Again, I'm hoping for banister cozies. The ivory inlay creeps me out far more than the funereal mask of a rich Egyptian kid."

"Amazing."

"The accounting ledgers—going back to the early 19th century—are in those low shelves under the portholes. So weird saying that. The books are under the portholes. I've been climbing up and down the ladder, rolling it along as I go, dusting the books. That top row up there is all crusty from old salt."

"Well," Baker said. "It's a ship. Salt spray and all that."

"Parts of the ship are all over the house—but mostly that turret door and here. I think the cabinets and cupboards in the big kitchen are strakes, too. A flair for the dramatic, had Whittie."

Baker ran his fingertips along an old leather book resting separately on a lectern. "Maybe he really did have a flare for decorating."

"The dark pink velvet drapes in one of the bedrooms upstairs scream 1950's Las Vegas strip casino. So, maybe. But again...the pink velvet is so out of here once we get the nod. I bet we can sell it on some antique fabrics marketplace. It is the real deal and I want it out so bad. Similar curtains hung in here—but I carefully took them down to get some more light in here. Can't see the dust in the dark."

Baker chuckled. "I spy with my little eye something that is *everywhere*."

Sanz giggled. "Ah, you see either dust or salt."

"The salt. What was he trying to keep out? Or in?"

"What do you mean?"

"Salt is used to ward off negativity in very basic spells."

"You know this, how? I thought he set the things out as a desiccant to protect his books from the ravages of old house draftiness."

"Salt has many magical properties, besides those of culinary avenues. I consider myself a pagan and fledgling witch. I read about this stuff all the time."

"Well, you will have a heyday here, Baker. There are more books about spells and incantations in this library than there is dust. Goliath is an occultist's paradise."

"I may never leave," he replied.

Sanz laughed. "The book there on the podium...that large leather tome of great musty odor and easily two thousand pages...it's a spell book. Uncle Albie's spell book. His Book of Shadows. His grimoire."

"I thought it was an old dictionary." He looked closely at the cover. "And here it is, the *Grimoire d' Albert Whitmore*."

Sanz took a few steps up a ladder. "Yep. Title is in French, and not another word is in anything I can read. He used a bizarre combination of Chinese and Latin. As if he were trying to confuse anyone who happened upon it."

"Confusion can be a useful tool." Baker's voice trailed off as he explored the heavy, yet intricate leather tome. "And one I have used to my advantage in the past."

She flipped on the Dustbuster. Its hum and sucking noise broke the otherwise very still quiet of the room.

Baker continued, speaking over the hum of the vacuum. "The Chinese is in a different hand. I mean, of course it is—unless Albie was fluent."

"In avarice, yes. Other languages, unknown."

———

Baker ran a single fingertip across the neatly written Chinese characters sandwiched in between the Latin text.

"The ink is different on the Chinese characters. The weight of the pen, too. It's like the person wrote the words on the dust of the paper. Lightly. Delicately. I like calligraphy." He flexed his fingers. The antique paper of the book made his fingers tingle. He tapped his middle finger against his thumb. It was not his fingertips that vibrated. It was characters he touched. Gave him goose-flesh. Made his skin crawl. Under his breath he whispered, "Powerful old beggar. What secrets are you hiding? It's not so hard to translate stuff." He whipped out his smart phone and took a few snaps. "I don't think this is parchment. Or vellum. It's unlike anything I've touched before. It rings with...evil."

"Going to google it?" Sanz asked from her perch. "If it is human skin, I think I don't want to know. And yes. Many things in this house have an aura of malintent."

Baker stepped back from the book and ran his fingers through his pink-tinged hair. "I am sweating. Gods, Sanz. What is this thing?" He paused for a moment, taking a deep breath. "Hey, why Sanz? Is that short for something?"

"Yes. My father's last name was Sanchez. He died when I was six. My given name is unused and best forgotten. It is Alberta. I am just another *Albert* in the long sordid line."

"Alberta. You are named after an entire province."

"You are to never, ever to refer to me by that name. Promise?"

"Sure. I can respect that."

Sanz continued. "There have been unfortunate and miserable deaths in the Whittie line for decades. Albert is a cursed family name. In 1886, the mother of Albie's sons drowned--my great-great-great-great grandmother. Her son, Lem Albert, died by electrocution in a New York subway around 1977. He left many spawn, of whom my mother is one by what we call Albert-6. My mother's name is Alberga. She was born four months after her father's untimely passing. Yes, he was producing children in his late 80's. She is three-quarters Chinese, one-quarter your basic Anglo mix. I am one-half Latina since Mom mated with Mr. Sanchez. My grandmother—Mom's mom was a lovely woman of questionable morals whose family was biological Chinese and fled to Hong Kong in the 1950's. I believe she was in her late twenties when she had Mom. That means that Albert-6 had a penchant for younger Chinese girls, on some level, as did the late, great Albert Sr. My mother was raised in a home where Chinese was never spoken above a whisper because it wasn't 'American.' Mom lit outta that twisted situation of body-part gambling and indentured servants working the family laundry and moved to Spanish Harlem. Fell in love with—Are you ready for this?—a man named Alberto. Another Albert. It is a curse. From what I understand, all Alberts have now passed, leaving only Mom and me. They all died. I am flummoxed and amazed that Albie's line continued though he banished his sons out of embarrassment. The paterfamilias himself, Albert Whitmore, succumbed to lung cancer and advanced old age and dementia—which I'm sure explains many of the items in this library. That is why I shall never be Alberta."

"Wicked. Maybe we can diagram that later. You know...a little tree with branches rising up from the Hell of Albert the First. Do you speak Spanish?"

"Speak, some. Yes. Read, no. My father was an awesome man who equated his native tongue with 'mean struggles.' So, he chose to speak English. I don't suppose you speak Latin or Chinese, do you?"

"I know people who do. The owner of the Chinese restaurant is fluent. I don't know if it's Mandarin or Cantonese or what script this is, but I'll show him the snaps. Latin can be machine translated. Praise be to Google."

"I like Chinese food."

"Let's go sometime. We can have a date. It keeps the conservatives happy when they see young couples frolicking in town. Gives them hope that they are safe from the ravages of reality. To keep things real I'll wear my pearls and you can wear combat boots. You have books to dust. Get on it, Cinderella."

"Killjoy."

Baker returned to the heavy pages, carefully tracing the Chinese characters again. "I know what this one is. I think." Keeping his fingertips on the somewhat recognized character and used his left hand to surf the web on his phone. "Yeah. It's the number three. Praise the countywide WIFI system offered gratis to all the gentry."

"One down, a million squiggles to go. I am not hopeful we shall ever uncover the secrets of Albert the First."

Baker giggled. "Oh, ye of little faith. *Three trees.* It's a name. A signature. *San Lin.*"

"Hail, Great-Great-Great-Great Granny," Sanz called.

Baker held the screen of his phone against the page and traced the characters with his fingertip again. He wanted to embrace them. Kiss them. Like a pilgrim at the feet of a statue of Christ. Or a groupie before a rock star. He wanted to genuflect. His heart thumped in his chest like he would die each time he resisted the urge to grow closer to the page. The whir of the hand-vac became a driving force behind him. Sanz's breaths, a wind at his back. The swirl of dust not caught up in the suction, a memory. He glanced nervously behind him then followed the urge—the compulsion to embrace the delicate calligraphy of the page. He lightly touched his lips to the parchment leaf.

He fell into a deep well. Cold—bitter cold—encompassed him. Pressure from an unrelenting torrent of water slammed into his chest wall, again and again. He smelled raw death. He tasted the Grim Reaper's sweat. He struggled to breathe. His ribs ached as if two hundred pounds sat atop him. He could not feel his legs. A moment of embarrassment passed quickly. He'd soiled himself. He'd pissed in the face of imminent demise. In the darkness, the wet blackness, he heard the mews of others as they succumbed to death's embrace. *I am not alone. I do not meet my end without witness. But they are so young. I would greet the road across the underworld without lantern or horse to prevent shared interment. Oh, and now it fades. The little ones...die.* Their final sounds faded until only the soft sound of flowing water and of his own breath filled the vestibule.

His legs were as confined and his body, though nearly frozen to the bone and sensations of flesh but memory, ached as if he'd taken a recent beating. *I am bone bruised. I am bloodied. He hurt me. Again. What did I do this time? Oh. I recall. I said no. No. A simple word that sealed my fate in this flooding mine shaft, the year of the boss' lord, eighteen hundred eighty-six.*

He smelled the sweet tobacco of his assailant's pipe as he remembered when he'd taken the blows. Indecent liberties had been taken with his body day after day. *Her body*. And when the vile act could not be completed due to too much drink or not enough time passed since the last offspring had been ushered into the world—there were beatings. He'd fought the advances. No. *She* had fought. These were not his memories. They were *hers*. She had taken the beatings. And now for love of simple human decency, drowned. *I am San Lin. Ancestors! Hear me! I call to you now as I die in this dark, foreign place. I have been violated, abused and cast aside like rubbish. I am your daughter, honorable ones. I seek you bring vengeance to my death that I may sleep easily and enjoy the offerings of my descendants.*

Baker allowed the still heavy, still clinging anguish and rage of San Lin to fill him. He saw with her eyes. Tasted with her mouth. Gagged upon the odors she inhaled. Five feet away were the dead bodies of those who had succumbed before her. Water-logged, bloated, eyes glassy and blank. But this was not San Lin's memory. This was a new action in the brain-play trance state he knew he endured. Not seen with her eyes. It was the eyes of the one who collected the bodies.

It wasn't the swim of the living. It was her spirit and it took all his strength to swim to the ladder. For the effort it took it might have been a mile not two arms lengths. There was no satisfaction given to lung or muscles. Oxygen fled. He touched the dilapidated ladder and pressed cheek against it as if it were a holy relic. This ladder meant life. A few seconds more of life. Nothing was so precious as that which could sustain breath.

Caught up in the vision, Baker silently crept to a shelf ladder opposite Sanz. He literally floated to the top with each foot against rung. As if play-acting, he dramatically took a deep breath, then exhaled. "Whitmore..." he whispered.

The ladder collapsed under his weight, and it flew out from underneath him. He clung to the twelve-foot-high bookshelf, the tips of his Doc Martens pushing books about five feet down for added stability. The ladder; the heavy, sturdy, old hardwood ladder, crashed against the closed pocket door creating a loud, deep thud. Where ladder met door the wood splintered. The ladder bounced and crashed again. The door rang with metallic clang. The door was a bell.

"What the...?" Sanz scrambled to the door. She ran her hand across the gouge in the wood where ladder had kissed door. "The door really is metal. It is freaking wood-encased bell metal. The book says it is steel. I don't think so." She reached into her front pocket and removed a small set of keys. She tapped the bronzish material peeking out from the tear in the wood. "Get down here, Baker."

She continued tapping. She pried off a little of the splintered wood from the door. "Check this out. This is copper and tin. The door is a bell."

Reeling from the jolt back to reality, Baker replied breathlessly. "I am more than just slightly precariously perched here, Sanz. Can you grab me another ladder or a chair or something? This is higher than I'd like to leap."

Sanz laughed. "I'm sorry. No leap of faith for you?"

"No, not today. And bells are another protective charm in witchcraft. Old Man Whittie was trying to make some magic up in here."

Sanz dashed to the far end of the library and pushed a second rolling ladder toward Baker. "All right, climb down and check this out."

She returned to the door and peeled away another layer of veneer and wood. "Mother is going to hate this. I'll have to glue the veneer back on somehow. Look...there are markings. Someone scratched something into the metal, hidden inside the wood. Dare I say we have a mystery here? Do you think I will get to pull a mask off the gardener to reveal the bad guy?"

"I'm fine, thank you. I was just possessed by the spirit of a drowned girl who had been repeatedly beaten and raped at the hands of whom I can only assume was Albert, but I'm fine. Don't worry about me. And those are runes. Like Viking runes. Holy Odin, Batman. He was desperate for protection."

Sanz cast a hard glance at Baker. "Possessed?"

"I touched the Chinese characters in the grimoire. They touched me back."

"F—"

"Yeah." Baker paused thoughtfully. "Yeah. Wow. She didn't die in an accidental flooding of a shaft after a cave in. She, and several others, were murdered. Drowned."

"There's documentation of the collapse. Newspaper records. Firsthand accounts of workers who escaped or were dug out. Old Man Albie took to bed for weeks after that, all broken up inside over the death of innocents. Look...I've got the article."

"I know what I saw. What I felt. And when has the media ever been truthful?"

"You have a point there." Sanz rifled around in an old wooden lateral file and pulled away a large flat of newspaper clippings. On the front cover of one was a picture of Whittie himself, flanked by a nurse in white with cap and what must have been his mine foreman. She read aloud, "Albert Whitmore incapacitated by melancholia after mine accident. Nursing team brought in from Seattle."

"I've seen this before. Local history book. That's his fire boss. You can tell by the big slab of chalk in his right hand. We studied this stuff in elementary school. Mostly just terms and such."

"Fire boss?" Sanz asked. "That's the guy who dies first, right?"

"Because he checks for poison gas before the workers go in. Would have used a canary or cat back then."

"Canaries and other little birds were ridiculously expensive. Albie bred his own. It's on another of his infamous lists contained in one of the all-knowing ledgers. Little birds." Sanz coughed. "Huh. Here's the original photo." She paused. "Huh. These are not the same. The original and the newspaper photos differ. It looks like a part of it was blurred out for publication." She held her hand over her mouth. "Oh, my God. Oh, my freaking God."

"What?"

"The fire boss. Holy...this can't be true. Dude isn't carrying a canary cage on his back." She paused, raising a hand to her forehead. "It makes sense now. They were all males. All of them."

"Okay, Sanz, what the heck are you talking about?"

"Albert's descendants. All the kids sent away to be raised by others. Boys. Not one daughter ever made it out of this house alive. What evil do I carry in my blood? Baker...the fire boss...he has a baby on his back. Why has no one noticed this before?" She answered her own question. "The newspaper carried an altered photo. Either the crime went undetected, or it was accepted and covered up. He owned the newspaper. He owned everything." She sighed, then voice quaking, continued. "The fire boss used babies." She pulled up a chair. "This is the kind of stuff that overwhelms me. I need to break it down into manageable segments."

"You do what you need to do."

"I learned a long time ago how to get myself sorted when my emotions run hot. When the information or situation before me is so charged it punches me in the gut —I step back. I need to quash emotion and just go with the facts. Not my first time at the rodeo, Baker. Just give me a moment and I'll logical myself into cognitive behavior. If I don't, then my synesthesia will push forward and I'll start smelling and hearing colors." Sanz closed her eyes and took several deep breaths, exhaling each one with deliberate force. "All the children of Albert sent back east were male. There are no records of females having ever even being born. But we all know there were girls born. The family has spoken about the curse for years. It's another fun topic at holidays."

"Curse?"

"None of the females directly sired by him survived. None. Rumor has it that Whitmore had a dozen concubines who produced lots of babies—both male and female. We can trace most of the male lineage. There are no direct maternal descendants." Sanz slumped over. "There are extant letters. Some are typed and signed. Some handwritten. In the largest of the ledgers—the ones that I have taken the time to read, he made list of physical properties. Of his chattel, including animals. You know...a dozen head of beef cattle, five hogs, including two lactating sows, forty goats and sheep, his fowl--

chickens, geese, turkeys...you get the idea. Then set off in the margin is a notation we took at face value. We all assumed, due to the expense, that he raised his own canaries. His 'little birds,' as he called them. Baker..." She paused. "The females born to him were his canaries. He killed them all. Why is this not common knowledge? How could it have been hidden?"

Baker doubled over. "They were slaves, Sanz. No one cared. I'm going to be sick."

"Door with the mirror on it off the foyer. Nearest bathroom." Sanz pointed toward the grand entrance hall.

Baker dashed toward the bathroom. He slammed the door behind him and tried to minimize the sounds of his gastric distress. After dry heaving and trying to sweat it out, he let loose with a hurl of tremendous proportions.

Sanz stood in the foyer, embarrassed for her new friend. "Are you okay?"

Baker grunted from behind the closed door.

Not knowing what else to say, she thought about what she wanted most after vomiting. "There's a pack of new toothbrushes under the sink. Help yourself." *Weird to say? I mean, really. What's more civil than giving a person a chance to clean up after something like that?*

A few moments later Baker emerged from the bathroom, pale, his brow covered in perspiration. "I'm sorry. It felt like someone punched me in the gut. Literally. Poltergeist activity here, much?"

"It happened to Mom once, too. She said it felt like she'd been Heimliched. We kind of laughed it off. In our family, we do have a tendency to ignore what we can't explain. Denial is big. Does that answer your question? This place is a hub of spiritualist activity. Why Old Albie built a séance room. I forgot to tell you about the séance room! It's kind of the same room as the cigars and brandy room—but it is definitely a room for metaphysical pursuits. It's off the smoking room. Like a closet."

"Most families are schooled in denial, Sanz. Your family more than most. In my case the 'pretending it didn't happen though it was untoward' was kind of what got me started into paganism. Mom laughed off my dreams—even though some of them occurred while I was awake. Nothing like telling your kid *you didn't really see that, honey.* Thanks for the toothbrush. Can I get something to drink?"

"Kitchen is this way," Sanz replied. "What kind of stuff did you see?"

"Lights around people's heads, shadows that had form and substance, things that appeared then disappeared. I swear, my parents can handle the fact I'm gender non-conforming better than they can my penchant for alternative spiritual beliefs."

"If you want to connect with spiritual things—that perhaps go bump in the night—
there's an old Ouija board upstairs."

"Sanz, I think you and I have been brought together for a higher purpose. This place—this house—the mines—the confusion between what truly happen, what folks think happen and what has been covered up—maybe we're supposed to bring clarity to the sordid history of Beacon Shores."

"Awesome! I *do* get to pull a rubber mask off the bad guy at the end. I've always wanted to do that," Sanz replied.

"*Scooby Doo* reference aside, that is exactly what it means."

CHAPTER TWO

Sanz led Baker to the main kitchen. The one too large for any family of less than twenty to stock, clean and maintain. Enormous copper pots hung in the center of the room above a huge brick oven. It had been constructed to feed a household of children and servants. Not slaves whose children were killed or moved across country.

Baker marveled at the brick oven. "Pizza."

Sanz laughed. "We haven't yet investigated it fully. It is too sooty inside and there must be six inches of ash. The oven is not the most impressive thing in the kitchen. Check this out..." she opened the stained-glass door before her. "This is the smaller pantry. It is larger than most apartment bedrooms. The shelves are each built from one, hand-hewn, redwood beam. They serve one very obvious purpose. No, it is not to shelve canned goods and warehouse boxes of oatmeal. These shelves are for the salt. Bag after bag of kosher rock salt, mind you. Three deep. A lifetime supply of salt. There is a 'salt-clause' in the will. I kid you not."

Baker walked to the end of the fully laden shelves. "Some of these containers are vintage. *Antiques Roadshow* would have a heyday in here."

"Every month we receive a shipment of salt directly from the Caster Brothers of Pennsylvania containing no less than three one-pound bags. We are supposed to refresh the dishes. We have not been keeping up with that." She paused and made a hand-vac motion and whir. "It really is in the will. And it's another non-negotiable expense. Mom and I joked about burning down the Caster Brothers salt house to end the contract, but there's something in the fine print that would send the standing order to its competition. Then we'd have to deal with Morton's. I can't handle beating down little girls with umbrellas, man. The logo and slogan weird me out. So, Mom and I gave up that diabolical plot."

"Next to the store-brand two-liter soda bottles is... salt. And nothing but salt. Huh. This place is full of surprises. I'd ask to explore a little more, but I feel like my insides have ruptured. Maybe I should wear some salt to protect myself from psychic harm."

Sanz reached into an open bag and palmed some salt. She sprinkled it on Baker's shoulders. "There. Safe to explore any haunted area of this god-forsaken place." She paused and caught Baker by the arm as he collapsed onto a crate. "Should we call your mom or something? You got sick."

"No. I'm all right. I still feel the energy—but it's okay. I'm a sensitive and empath. I know things. Albert...he was a very bad man. He did give children to his fire boss. He did. I see it like a movie playing before my eyes. He used newborns. His children by the Chinese girls. He saved the sons and shipped them off because of the power of his bloodline and used the daughters as the canaries. He married San Lin to get her dowry. She hated him."

"What a sick son of a...Look, Baker—maybe I should get you out of this place. You have a seriously dire pallor."

"Ask your mom if I can spend the night."

Sanz laughed. "Hello? What? This house is making you sick. Why would you want to spend the night?"

"I am a glutton for punishment. I enjoy playing Russian roulette. I am a fire walker. Sword swallower. A human cannonball. I order *Fugu* at Japanese restaurants."

"Pick one from category A and two from category B, huh? Fine, whatever. Mother won't care if you spend the night, nor do I suspect your mother will balk at the idea."

"Yes. True. Mom knows I don't fool around—no alcohol or drugs. No bleeding chickens in a pentagram. No rolls in the hay. Sharing that part of myself seems like way too much commitment. I can barely perceive my own *wyrd*—fate—much less tie mine to another's. I'll text Mom. I remain purposely celibate. To be honest, I haven't met anyone who inspires me to carnal acts as of yet."

"You're a virgin, too?" Sanz asked. "I, unlike a few of my high school friends, did not do the deed in Daddy's car on prom night. I wasn't interested. Then."

Baker nodded as he texted his mother. "Mostly. Messed around a couple of times. Didn't insert tab A into slot B. I've had both male and female special friends. And I understand wanting to wait. Seriously."

Sanz looked up from her phone. "*Wyrd* as in karma?"

"Yes. When you lay with another, you accept part of them into your core being. I have enough baggage on my own being gender expansive in a binary society. I don't need someone else's karma riding shot gun." Baker paused. "All right. I'm staying here tonight. I'd like to return to the library, if we may. Can we sleep there?"

"On a dirty chaise. Sure."

"Yes, but my new best friend, Sanz, has a hand-vac."

"But does she do windows?"

"Should we take provisions? More salt? Holy water? A sigil against murderous pedophiles?"

Sanz chuckled. "Again, it's choose one from column A and one from column B and batten down the hatches. Let's make some sandwiches and popcorn or something. I think we've got some outrageously sugary cereal Mom bought when she was PMSing, too. One bowl of that and you will be wired for sound. Oooo...we've got some frozen pizzas, too."

"Pizza it is. Hey, what's this?" Baker reached for a black box tucked under a back shelf.

"It is a box. You've discovered another box! The house is filled with such things."

"Do any others have a Tudor Rose engraved on them?"

"I know what that is. It's a symbol of two houses, joined. Henry VII."

Baker lifted the box and blew off a thin layer of dust. "This heavy black box has a Tudor Rose engraved on the top, bottom and sides. It does represent two royal houses made one and some say deeper meanings of a goddess and the fae. It's a pentacle of protection for whatever is in the box. Rose lore also includes the *sub rosa* context. It represents a secret."

"You know, Baker, displaying such witchy knowledge in a haunted house might get you a cup of hot chocolate. Tell me more."

"Do you know what wood this is?"

"It's black. Black wood. Wood that is black of color. I skimmed over some of the inventory, to be honest."

"Check it, Sanz. It's a gorgeous piece. It's got to be catalogued." Baker left the pantry with the box and slid into a bench seat in the breakfast nook.

"Probably." Sanz opened the pdf reader on her phone and thumbed through the table of contents. "Incidentally, you are sitting at the shelling table, a place where various vegetables were removed from their skins, husks and peels. This table is constructed from Major Oak, the famous tree from Sherwood Forest. It's in the inventory." She paused, scrolling. "Box. Wood. Black. Decorated. Yes. It's here. It's Irish bog oak. And yes, that is a Tudor Rose."

"Any indication of the contents? Or where the key is located?"

"It's under the rose—so it's a secret. Contents unknown. Keys are problematic, as we've discussed. We have no idea where the key box is. Nor do the attorneys, caretakers, service station attendant or clerk at the convenience store."

"Bog oak and a Tudor Rose Pentacle. I can open this." Baker paused. "Sanz, can I pick the lock?"

"Heck, if you can pick this one, I'll let you try the turret door."

"Any tools?"

Sanz opened the 1960's style refrigerator and removed two bottles of water. She set them on the table and then stood before a large bank of drawers that took up an entire section of the kitchen wall. "There are tools, yes. Lots of tools. There are duplicates of tools. Triplicates. Someone hit every yard sale in town for decades, and never had one of their own. I mean, how many ball pein hammers does one person need?"

"Depends upon how many ingrates needs beaten into submission on any given day. What I need something small and thin. Like an eyeglass repair kit screwdriver."

"Junk drawer!" Sanz reached inside a long, narrow drawer. "Yes, we have that. And it's ours. This dollar store eyeglass repair kit is owned by the Sanchez family. Use it wisely."

Baker took the eyeglass repair kit from her hands reverently. "I am honored to have access to your tiny flat head screwdriver."

Sanz laughed and made the sign of the cross before him. "May you be blessed."

Baker held the black box at an angle to get just the right amount of light on the lock. "Oh, yeah. I can open this. Question is...should I?"

"Yo, Baker, this is kind of your department, me not being all up on witchy magic stuff, but are not the contents of that box protected from the outside?"

"It does appear so, yes."

"It's probably just more salt. An emergency salt supply, safe from the degradation of the time and humidity."

Baker chuckled. He had inserted both the Philips head and flat head eyeglass screwdrivers into the antiquated lock and busily channeled a safe cracker. He cursed under his breath.

Sanz tapped her foot nervously. "I hate waiting."

"Patience is a virtue, is it not?" Baker replied. "I don't want to break this, so let me take my time."

Sanz growled. A low, throaty growl like an angry cat. "So are magnificence and liberality."

Baker didn't look up, but replied softly, "Most folks

need more liberality. The quality of being open to new ideas and free from prejudice is lost on so many."

She spun around in a circle and wandered into the main kitchen. "I'll stay out of your hair."

Baker continued his sharp focus. A bead of sweat rolled off his brow. He wiped it away with the back of his hand and heard a "click." He pushed again and the antique clasp sprang open. "Victory is mine!"

Sanz rushed back to the little kitchen. "You got it!"

Baker used both hands to lift the unsealed lid. It creaked from disuse, the hinges tight with age. "What do you hope to find inside?"

"Is this a game of *what is the best that could happen*?" Sanz asked.

"Sure, let's go with that. Given the history of this place you might want to ask what is the worst that could happen, too."

"The best that could happen is that there is something inside that says we can sell this place and all its macabre contents and move away. No offense intended. So far you are the bright center of Beacon Shores. And we could totally embrace a social media relationship if I move."

"No offense taken. Let's go with second best before I lift out this fine piece of red velvet and unwrap whatever has been safely hidden for who-knows-how-long."

"The key to the room under the witch's cap."

"And the worst?" Baker's fingertips touched the velvet bundle.

"Salt."

The bundle had been artistically tied into a knotted shape that resembled a lotus blossom. "Well, this is interesting. There is salt." Baker paused and took up the second object long hidden in its velvet shroud. "And a key. A key of gold. I doubt this is brass."

"Wow. Just, wow." Sanz placed her hands atop Baker's shoulders. "It might just be it, Baker. The key that unlocks my new bedroom."

Baker blew salt off the old, oddly shaped key and passed it to Sanz.

She squinted and held it up to the light. "It has little itty bitty Chinese characters on it. Never seen that on a skeleton key before. Look." She displayed the key's shank to Baker. "I'm pretty game to try this puppy out. If nothing else, it's a sweet looking key and I'm sure it will unlock something. Maybe more than one something. That would make it the first key to unlock anything in this behemoth mansion."

"Why keep it wrapped in a locked box, in salt-encrusted velvet?"

"Welcome to my nightmare, Baker. Let's away to the turret, shall we?" Sanz patted him on the shoulder and motioned for him to follow her. "We can sneak up the back stairs." She turned off the oven. "The pizza can resonate while we explore. Just turning the oven off for safety's sake. It'll cook. Thing is hot."

"This place is a labyrinth," Baker replied. He closed the box.

"A labyrinth eventually comes to a head dead center. This is a maze, which makes us uncertain of which path leads to the treasure or certain doom." Sanz opened a non-descript wood panel door on the far end of the main kitchen. Its rusty hinges creaked as she forced it ajar. "And mythologically speaking, the labyrinth was home of the Minotaur—an unpleasant beast."

Baker stared at the incredibly narrow passage. "Ah,

but the word maze is a thirteenth century word meaning delirium or delusion. Those are pretty big monsters, too." He coughed. "I am not going to fit." Beyond it was most certainly the steepest stairwell he had ever seen. "There is no banister, and this is more a ladder than stair."

"You'll be fine. Just think of how nimble the servants must have been back in the day to run this sucker several times a day waiting on the old man and his various guests. The séance room is upstairs in the men's study. Brandies and cigars after dinner will be served in the salon while one of the girls plays piano forte."

"That kind of crudes me out. He used slaves for entertainment. Just freaking wrong. On many levels."

"I don't mean to make light of things, but I'm pretty sure that's exactly what occurred in the dark recesses of this fine collection of sins. It was probably worse than I can imagine. I don't like to think about the suffering of those kids. My own four times grandmother. Come on." Sanz scampered up the stairs using the walls to balance herself.

Baker took the steps a bit more gingerly. The rise and run of the treads were all off. Short. As if no one in the mid-1800's had a foot size greater than six. He wore size eleven. Half his foot hung off each step. "Hail the beloved dead. How many steps to the second floor?"

"About a hundred. If these steps were built to modern specifications, maybe forty. There is some weird shit scrawled along the wall near the top."

"Chinese characters?"

"No. More like stick figures. Pictures."

The lighting cast scary shadows before them as they slowed their pace near the top. "Electricity was an afterthought. The entire ceiling here is caked with soot.

The servants used candles. This is another place where Mom stands and sighs. The peak of this staircase must be twelve feet up. And there's no room for a ladder or anything. If she can ever get the ceiling cleaned, it will be a miracle."

"I find it hard to believe that servants could manage these stairs at all. I mean, sure...some of them were kids, but what about the portly matron who acted as head of the house?"

"She used the lift. The elevator."

Baker stopped. "There's an elevator? I am climbing steps that are half the size of my foot and there is an elevator?"

Sanz giggled. "It doesn't always work. Sometimes it goes down instead of up or gets stuck between floors. It is far creepier to use that old lift than walk up a soot-filled, windowless, miniature staircase."

"Does it go to the lower levels?" Baker asked. "This place is atop an old mine. Can you get to the shaft?"

"I've not explored what lies below too intently, Baker. Mom isn't keen on me playing in the dirty history of our new home. She is in denial, big time." Sanz paused. "Ah, here. Look. Maybe. If you can. The scribbles."

"There is no way I can look over you or under you or around you. I am quite squished in the confines of this back-kitchen staircase."

Sanz motioned for Baker to wait. "I'll open the door at the top, step out of this delightfully cramped stair and then you can look at the lovely drawings left by the hand of children or desperate adult and tell me what you think." She pushed against the diminutive door at the top of the flight of steps. The smooth wood had worn down over the years and the place where one should push was readily apparent. "A hundred hands over a hundred years," she whispered. "Empty all the salt dishes to allow spirits full entry. I think that's the curse. It's been over a hundred years since the subjugation of children in this place and now...the curse is coming to light. Maybe."

Baker knelt where Sanz had stood to look at the drawings. "These are scratched. Not drawn."

"There's a plaque in my room—bolted to the wall above the door. It says *a hundred hands over a hundred years to make a house a home.* As if this place would ever be a home. It is a monstrosity of epic proportion. It's probably the oddest thing about this place. It was never a home. It was a prison."

"Albie must have wanted whomever it was who used your room at one time to learn a lesson. One that is lost on me." Baker pulled out his cell and took a snap of the etchings. "I need to look at these when not on my knees in a poorly lit stairwell."

"My evil plan unfolds. I knew I could get someone else interested in solving all the mysteries of this place. Like I said...I just want to pull the rubber mask off the bad guy."

Baker took the last few steps hunched over and didn't stand upright until he was through the doorway. "Can I slide down the banister on the way down?"

"Sure. Only it's not smooth and the effects of the carved ripples will likely leave you very sore. You may be genderfluid, but your body is male. Ouch. Yanno?"

"Good safety tip. I don't have body dysmorphia. I like things the way they are. Not going to scuff the family jewels. I will use the stairs."

"All righty then. Now that our escape has been planned, I dare say it's time for us to climb the final flight to the witch's cap. If we get in there, I am so moving all my stuff. I made a new friend with muscles. Think he'd help?"

"There is another narrow-ass staircase?" Baker wiped his brow. "I am in prime physical condition and I am sweating. I don't like sweating, Sanz."

"Think of it as training for your weightlifting competitions. Or video games."

"How can you tell I play?" Baker asked.

"You have classic wrist-shake-out syndrome. You do it unconsciously, I think."

Baker chuckled. "You don't miss a thing, do you?"

"That has yet to be proved. This way, shall we?"

Sanz led Baker along a long, curved corridor, dark from the walnut paneling and stained-glass lamp shades. Artwork hung from picture rails and occasional tables graced the chair rail every ten feet or so. Chinese vases and carved *objets d'art* adorned the tables. Well placed crushed velvet chairs dotted the highly polished wood floor so black it shone like a mirror. Around the curve a heavily draped window allowed only a miniscule amount of sunlight to shine into this grand corridor.

"Can we open the curtains?" Baker asked.

"Oh, God, no. You'll see all the dust. And in the light of day we'd probably find more dishes of salt. I can't deal with that right now. I am developing an aversion to foil ashtrays filled with sodium chloride." She pointed at a door. "This is the séance room. Technically, the upstairs parlor or something. A gentlemen's spiritual retreat, maybe. I don't know, exactly. There is art of questionable taste in there. The literature about this place says it is Pre-Raphaelite. Bosomy women and knights in armor and pristine Anglo religious iconography of the Holy Family when we all know that Mary, Joseph and Jesus had brown skin and black hair. I love misrepresentation. It's my favorite."

"Not to make a detour, but I would like to see that room," Baker replied.

"Yes—mostly certainly. After we see if this key opens the room under the witch's cap."

"It will. I know it will."

Sanz pressed on a panel next to a decorative wall beam.

"Huh. This large column...is that a flying buttress?" Baker asked.

"No. This is a not a flying buttress. But, it is a support beam and by pushing on the wall to the left, a secret door is revealed." The panel popped open with another hard nudge. "And this is how the other half lived a hundred years ago. Secret panels in the wall that lead to awesome turret rooms."

"While subjecting immigrant children to tortures beyond the pale."

"Total killjoy there, Baker. Would you like to lead the way? The light pullcord is tacked to the wall. Old school. Seems someone wanted a bit of illumination shed on this corner of horror. The lightbulb is ancient, yet functional and tied off to a bent nail. We haven't followed the cotton wire yet to find where it connects to the main electricity. Which remember, was an afterthought in this place."

Baker sighed, then breezed past Sanz and through the non-descript panel. He felt for the cord and gave it a pull. A single bare bulb flickered on, barely illuminating the second narrowest staircase he'd ever seen. "Another ladder to climb, huh?"

"Not as steep. Not as many steps. Up at the top,

there's a trapdoor thing. Push up and climb out onto the catwalk. You're probably tall enough to see out the windows. I, alas, am not."

"Aces." Baker began the climb up the steps. "I walk on unfamiliar ground, my friend. Perhaps you should have gone first."

"No. I want the monsters to eat you first. Will give me time to flee." Sanz giggled. "I guess, in this house, the builder was the monster and it's the spirits of those he abused that will turn us all inside out."

"You offer such comforting words, Sanz. You know my head and stomach are churning from the fierce energies of this place, right? You want me to go headfirst into the abyss when I might hurl. I should have never approached you all friendly like as you bemoaned your plight at the beach. You are truly evil."

"Yeah, yeah, yeah. Get up there." Sanz scurried through the trap door after Baker. "I love it up here."

"It's clean," Baker said as he peered out the lower half of the east window.

"In anticipation of having the locksmith over, Mother asked me to dust and mop and all that. I even did the windows. Because this is going to be my room. If the key opens the cap."

Baker allowed the grandeur of the solid wood wall to envelope him. "This is impressive. That's gold, huh?" He ran his fingers across the large, intricately detailed filigree lock. "Do you have a futon or something that can be easily carried up that stairway?"

"I'll figure something out. We still don't know what's under the witch's cap. I mean, we can tell it's another six to eight feet up—so probably more stairs, and the space under the cap is at least twelve by twelve. So, it's large enough above to be a bedroom..."

"But perhaps too narrow below to get anything into it." Baker stepped aside and waved Sanz forward. "Let's do this thing."

Sanz took a deep breath and exhaled forcefully. "We thought about getting a drone and peeking in from the outside. However, if this key opens the turret, I wonder if Mom will give me the money she would have otherwise spent on the locksmith to decorate. That would be sweet." She held the key firmly before her and slid the bit of the key into the lock. The lock accepted the bit, the shoulder and the shank of the key. It fit all the way to the bow. She paused before rotating it, one hand pressed firmly against the oak and ironwood wall. The key turned easily. The key turned nearly 360 degrees. The lock clicked and popped. "Oh, dear God. It worked. Did it work? I think it's unlocked."

"Open the door, Sanz. That's the only way we'll know for certain. I want to help you decorate your new room. I love textiles and fabric samples. Cashmere gives me goosebumps. And those Sherpa/velveteen comforters? Love them. It's like rolling up in a hug." Baker cleared his throat. "Open it."

Sanz slid her fingers under the latch and pulled it out. The door opened with a whoosh of dust. It creaked on its brass and gold hinges and the weight of the steel and ironwood strakes fought against its own ancient inertia. She stood in the partially open door and looked around for a light fixture. "Wow. Just, wow."

"What?" Baker asked straining to look around Sanz.

"Welcome to a part of the manor untouched by modern convention. Baker, there are wall sconces here.

For candles. And cobwebs a foot thick. And chains. There are chains affixed somewhere higher. They're training down the wall. What did he do up here? There's no electricity wires that I can see. How the hell does the light go on and off?"

"Want me to go first and knock the cobwebs away?"

"I can go under them. I totally need to Hoover up here. And ask Mother to get an electrician. This is like a cell."

"Here, let me pass. I am not afraid of cobwebs."

Sanz stepped back and allowed Baker to go before her. "I'm not afraid of cobwebs. I just don't like crawly things against my skin. Although I haven't tried it, I'm sure I would not enjoy the sensation of cotton candy against my cheeks, either."

"Pansy." Baker waved his arm and took down what may have been a century's worth of cobwebs from the entrance to the steps leading to the room under the witches cap. "Come on. It's not so bad. And these stairs are far better than that first flight."

Sanz scampered up behind him. "Mother is going to thrilled."

There were a dozen steps. High above him Baker could clearly see the rafters, eaves, and dormers comprising the peaked cap on the turret. It had no windows, but rather small slits of leaded glass along its top parameter. "I can see the top, Sanz. We've made it!"

"I am so freaking excited. I am totally going to have a meltdown if I don't find my calm." She twirled around the small room as soon as she entered it. She envisioned herself dancing in a long skirt with layers of petticoats underneath. And high button shoes. She stopped dead in her tracks when she noticed Baker. His posture *screamed* pain. His face had grown pale. Sallow.

"It feels funny up here," he said softly. "The air is wrong. It's thick. Stale."

"Baker? Dude. Are you all right? You look funky." He had his chin tucked into his chest. He raised his head just enough to shoot her a glare colder than the room. She felt the emotions of pure contempt wrap themselves around her like a dirty sheet.

She followed the round wall around until she stood next to her friend. The room went cold. No insulation. No outlets. Broken furniture cast to one side. One stained glass window was cracked.

And then Baker spoke. "Please, no more. Please don't make me work in the mine today, yes? I cook you stew and bread you like instead." It was Baker's voice—but not Baker. The words sounded foreign coming from his mouth. It wasn't the childlike Asian accent. It wasn't the tonal inflection. It wasn't Baker. It wasn't him speaking. Period.

"Dude? What's going on?" she asked.

Baker reached out and touched her shoulder. A simple gesture. A non-threatening gesture. The aftershock of the touch pushed her back hard. Hard onto her backside. Knocked the wind from her.

Her head swimming, Sanz pulled herself upright. "If I allow you to cook for me you'll just eat it all before it is served, you greedy little thing." She found she could barely breathe. Her extremities felt leaden and her middle section ached with a burning sensation. She wore a large, heavy costume, the mask of which blocked her true vision and speech. A mask of power. *I have power. I have great, all-encompassing power. Over this girl. Over everything.* "You work the mine today, Lin. I'll hear no more of it. Has not your time on your leash made you more compliant?" Her mouth uttered words over which she had no control. She was in a dream and a demon moved her voice to speak.

Baker knelt. "Baby come soon. I cannot pull weight. Fire boss will beat."

Sanz spit. Her mouth tasted of chaw. It turned her stomach. But not so much as the words streaming from her mouth. "It's probably another girl. All of you have given me nothing but girls. I don't care what happens to you, or the baby." Sanz could not believe the words coming from her lips. "Go to the shaft. Give me a full day's work or I will leave you here. Chained to the wall and seal you up with your precious ancestors."

"No!" Baker screamed as his body moved against his will. He could not stop. He flew at Sanz and pummeled her. Fists, feet, kicks, bites. Sanz was down and he continued. Sanz was bloodied. And still, he continued. "I shall not work in mine today! My time is soon. I will not have baby in mine shaft."

Flat on her back, the spirit of her forefather Albert Whitmore plaguing her, Sanz laughed. A cold, hard belly laugh. "It's the strop for you, girl. Even in your confinement I shall not spare the rod for a spoiled child."

Lin thrust her left hand against Albert's face. "I am wife! You marry me legal. I make my own decision as lady of the house."

The blow didn't faze him. "Lady of the house?" Sanz rose. She wiped blood from her face with the back of hand. "Lady of the house? You are nothing but a glorified belly warmer. You are a slave. A slave. It is of no consequence that there is a legal binding between us that calls me husband and you wife. I wed you to gain control over your family's land in China and in the South Pacific. What is the name of that island? Hawaii. It was your dowry and your father deeded it willingly. For all intents and purposes, I am God to you."

"You are nothing to me." Baker spat. The issue of Albert Whitmore rolled inside. He felt the fluttering heartbeat and strong life force of San Lin's child. "I jump, Albert. I jump from ledge. I will not be your slave. No longer."

"You are a plucky little thing. I knew that when I first saw you." Sanz felt her face swell from the blows she'd taken. "All right. Go to the kitchen. Today, you shall not work in the mine. But in your stead, four others shall. The youngest of the young. It's high time they learned how to carry a lantern or use a bellows."

Lin shuddered. The little ones...they could not go to the mine. The dark, dank, unforgiving mine. One wrong step and they'd be goners. That's what the fire boss called the dead. *Goners.* "Little ones do not work in the dark. They sort the black at the end."

"Not today. If you will not go to the mine, they will. Those little girls—they will work the mine and they will learn how to cook my food and take care of my personal needs. Little half-breeds will take better direction than you ever have. I should have never brought over help from China. Stubborn people. But not so much as the Irish." He was talking to himself now.

"Those girls—they are too young to do the things you say. They are the daughters of your foreman and fire boss by my aunties. Their light skin and eyes cannot save them. Better they became your birds than what you would do to them. What you do to me. It is a bad thing."

"I have warned you never to speak of my canaries. The little birds are our secret here at the manor."

Lin clenched her fists. This was it. This was her final hour. She felt the tug of her ancestors and the crushing weight of a short, hard life pressing against her. "You take babies—girl babies—fresh from their mother's breast and you make them breathe the bad air in the new channels. You are too cheap to buy expensive birds from East Coast and send them on train. Instead you make goners of your daughters and the daughters of your crew. I speak the truth. I know the truth. I have buried the babies. I give them names and say the words. I do not say the Church words. I remember the Chinese prayers and I say them. I call to their ancestors to claim them, though they are girl children."

Albert lashed out and grabbed her throat. His large hand encircled her neck. He squeezed. "Do not speak of such things." He raised his left hand and brought it crashing down against her head. Lin went limp from the blow, unconscious. "Well, looks like we'll never know if you carry a son or a daughter. For today, San Lin, my little rebel, you shall be dealt with most harshly."

Sanz snapped out of the haze the possession by the spirit of Albert in which she had been ensconced. She had collapsed. And Baker, too. He had curled up into a fetal position.

CHAPTER THREE

"Baker? Baker, are you all right?" Sanz crawled to him and pulled his head into her lap.

"I'm okay. Can I just rest here for a moment?"

Sanz stroked Baker's hair. "I just got jumped by something really nasty. I need a shower. I need to bleach my brain."

"Albert. It was Albert. And San Lin spoke through me. We acted as conduits. Channels. For memories. I wonder how often these events play out with no one sensitive enough to acknowledge their presence. Ghosts cycling through the terrors of their lives without witness or reprieve."

"Albert is a royal pain in the butt. He is haughty and completely oblivious to the pain he causes—he caused—others. If it doesn't serve him, it does not exist. If it didn't serve him. Past tense. This is strange. It feels as though it was happening in current time—but I get that this is all memory. Poor San Lin. And what about the others? I need a serious DNA cleanse. Is there such a thing?"

"You may want to reconsider using this room. Bad things happen up here. Bad things that left bad memories. This was where he went to rape them, beat them and pass judgement. I think he brought them here—because it's so far up no one could hear their screams. Under the witch's cap. Abject, unstoppable suffering and death under the witch's cap. Sanz...this was where he and his men assaulted them. Bound and gagged them. Chained them to the wall and hurt them. Those I-bolts and the C-rings affixed to the studs and the twelve-foot-long chains...Sanz...this place ended so many. They were kids, Sanz. Little girls."

Sanz choked out her words. "Though his evil permeates this house, to its foundation and beyond into the mine shafts and tunnels, this room—this small barren room with its ornate door is where he sentenced five girls to die. He forced them down the sub-basement shaft. He bolted them to the floor. He broke the dam to the bay and flooded a passage through the mine. Their lives meant nothing to him. He had other workers. Other young women he could exploit."

The stillness and shock of the events under the witch's cap broke as Sanz's mother bellowed up the long staircase. "Sanz? What the hell are you doing?"

"I found the key, Ma. Baker and I are checking things out."

"Who's Baker?"

"We're coming down," Sanz called. "Baker, do I look like I've just been bashed around by a dead relative?"

He shook his head. "Do I?"

"We're okay. She won't question me if everything looks in place."

Baker smoothed an errant strand of hair to a position

behind her left ear. "You're okay. I could be perfectly fine if I never experienced something like this again." *But I know better. It's hitting me hard.*

Baker and Sanz found Alberga covered in soot and dust at the bottom of the staircase. "Mom, this is Baker. Local boy. Baker, this is Bergie, my mom. She is not usually covered household grime." Sanz leaned toward her mother. "Not your best look, Ma."

"Nice to meet you, Baker."

"Thank you, ma'am. Nice to meet you, too."

"Ma, Baker found the key in the big pantry inside an old box. He picked the lock. Didn't break anything."

"I thought there was pretty much only salt in the pantry. And in every box. And drawer, dish and upright receptacle."

Sanz laughed. "There was salt. But also, a key."

"Another of Albert's asinine spells to keep an object hidden in plain sight?" Bergie asked, taking the key from her daughter. "I am not in the mood to explore the tip top recesses of this house. What's up there?" She examined the key, then returned it to Sanz.

Baker replied softly, "Memories."

"Well, all right. I'm fine with those swirling around up there. I'm sick of dust and salt."

Sanz chimed in. "Dust only. No salt.

"Better than the east wing. You two warming up a pizza in a cold oven?"

"His mom already said he could spend the night." Sanz glanced upward at her mom, putting out a feeler for response emotion.

"Aren't you a little old for boy-girl sleep overs? I thought the cut-off was puberty for that sort of thing."

"It's okay, Ma. Baker is purposely celibate, and you

know me—my interest in romance is nil. We're going to sleep in the library. Pocket doors wide open."

"Baker, you're wearing black eyeliner and a kilt. And your roots are showing. How long has it been since you dyed your hair pink? Who's your hairdresser? God knows I need my roots done, too. Is she in town?"

"I am gender nonconforming, ma'am. I identify as male for societal reasons. At this point am not experiencing sexual feelings toward either sex. Haven't found the right person yet. I am happy with myself. My hairdresser is one town over at I'd Dye for You Salon."

"It is refreshing to see such maturity in a young person. You two have fun."

Sanz had kind of been holding her breath waiting for her mother's reply. She exhaled forcefully. "Thanks, Ma."

Bergie walked away, mumbling to herself. She turned, "I'm cancelling the locksmith."

"Yes, Mom," Sanz said. She turned to Baker. "Our evil plan unfolds."

"Séance room available for use?" Baker asked.

"Yep. Let's pull that pizza and get some drinks and go sit a spell. Commune with restless spirits of this place."

"Do you know what you're asking for?"

"The end of boredom. The end of a family curse by bringing light to heinous crimes and sins of the past. Proof—we have that. The photo of the fire boss."

"Only proves he had a baby on his back. Doesn't prove he put it there at Albert's request for use as a predicter of foul air."

"Fine. Let's find proof. I feel like making it rain justice all up in here."

CHAPTER FOUR

Non-descript mostly cooked frozen pizza and sodas balanced against the incline of the stairs, Baker and Sanz made their way to the grand hall, wherein rooms were hidden behind solid-looking panels of walnut, oak, blackwood and decorated with ivory inlay and silk wallpaper.

Baker took note of the contrast of old world and new. The gaudy plastic pizza tray with its pseudo-Italian colors, printed in China no doubt, clashed orange and bright green and yellowish white against the regal properties of the finely milled hardwoods and animal body part decorations. "I'm so glad they don't build them like this any longer," he said.

"Word. All these exotic, extinct woods and the ivory alone make me ill. It's not like I want everything constructed from straw and mud, but this is too much. It brings new levels to being depraved and greedy." She counted wall panels going right. "One, two, three, four... the fifth is the door."

"It looks like a wall."

"Yes, well, they liked to keep their fine collection of sins private. Secret." She pressed the heel of her hand against the center of the four by sixteen wall panel. It clicked and opened. "It's a bit narrow, but just turn sideways. Big bellied rich men back in the day probably had another entrance, though I haven't found it yet. Maybe in the east wing. I don't know."

"Something to add to our list." Baker rotated the pizza tray so that he could pass it to Sanz then followed her into the room. "You have land in Hawaii?"

"Yeah. And other places. Part ownership of a closed lime mine on one of the San Juan Islands and a marina called Roche Harbor that was leased to the county for some ungodly length of time."

The study was windowless. Gaudy. Ornate. Not musty, but permeated with the odor of alcohol, sweet tobacco, sweat, tears, and fear.

Baker sighed. "It's clean. And Sanz, there's a really funky smell in here. It's semen. A hundred-year-old spunk from sick old men who thought they ruled the world."

"That is disturbing."

Baker pulled a satin seat-covered iron and wood chair up to a small round table upon which he'd set the pizza.

"We must keep all furnishings intact, so sayeth the last will and testament, and I guess the odors that come with the house. Totally rank. It's this room. Something isn't right. It's not square. Do you understand? It is off kilter, somehow."

Baker lifted a piece of thin crust pizza and blew on it. "This whole place is out of whack. I've never smelled such foul odors in one place in my entire life. It's like walking into a 1970's porn shop."

"I've been in here before. It wasn't like this before. Something has changed."

Baker chewed silently and studied the corners of the room. He mumbled through a half-chewed slice. "I got it. Far wall, lower left corner nearest the harpsichord. The floor is wrong. The wall isn't right."

Sanz lifted a slice of pizza. "It's a pianoforte not a harpsichord, and yes. I see it now. It's like someone didn't close a door all the way, leaving it ajar. An entire wall, ajar." She set the slice down and dialed her mother on her cell. "Ma, did you find the main entrance to the stinky old men room today? Not the secret panel door." She listened as her mother spoke. "Okay, thanks." She ended the call. "Mother did not visit this room today. In fact, Mother did not, emphatically. She has a few choice words for the east wing that I shall not repeat."

They approached the corner, squeezing under the forerunner of the modern-day piano. Sanz poked at the buckle where wall met floor. "Who was in here?"

"And how do we open the wall?"

Sanz ran her palms against the dark grain of the wall. "This is not wood. It's more like canvas." She'd lived long enough in the house to know that doorknobs weren't always the sign of exit and egress. "Let me run through that pdf. That's how I found out about the skinny door to this room."

Baker continued searching for the reason behind the funky corner of the room. "Is this like a gym curtain?" He poked the heavy canvas. "This is the most marvelous example of *trompe l'oeil* I've ever seen. Think of it as antique 3-D art."

She pinched her fingers and spread them across the screen of her phone to enlarge the text. "All right.

Smoking room. Sealed." She paused. "This room is not sealed. It just doesn't have a door." From her squatting position, she fell onto her bottom and let her left hand hit the side of the pianoforte. The instrument clanged as if plucked.

Baker startled. "Sanz. Do that again."

"What?"

"Touch the piano—where you did it before."

Sanz frowned. "I'm not big on listening to the plucking of strings from underneath. It sounds tinny and hollow to me. Did you know that a piano strikes a chord while a pianoforte, plucks?"

"You are a wealth of information, Sanz. But truly... when you touched the piano, the wall trembled," Baker replied.

"Well, that is not in the guidebook." She placed flat palm against the side of the pianoforte, her eyes on Baker's hand, which he'd placed flat against the canvas wall.

And the wall quivered. Quivered like a water disturbed by a pebble.

Baker gasped. "No way."

"I saw that."

Baker lifted his palm and shook his hand out. "What is behind curtain number one? This extremely well-designed, two-dimensional illusion of a three-dimensional fake wall."

"What correlation does the piano have to the wall? And W.T.F. is this wall?" She lifted her hand again and touched fingertips only to the keys. A dank clang came from inside the instrument, and the wall rippled—ever so slightly.

Baker stood and pushed the piano. Heavier than it

looks, he moved it about a foot. Sanz caught herself looking at his carved biceps. "Need help?"

"No problem." He paused. "I wonder if H.H. Holmes helped design this house."

A great cacophony of angry strings rebelled, and the ancient veneer threatened to snap. She closed the lid quickly to mute the noise. "What the heck? The piano is haunted, too?"

"I don't know about that—but look. Look at the wall." Baker grabbed Sanz's arm to get her attention away from the rebellious pianoforte. "Sanz."

She turned and nearly toppled. "It's..."

Baker finished her sentence. "Gone."

"How did Albert create a wall that disappears when the piano is touched? And why? I don't recall reading any notations about the architect for this place, but Old Albie was just as diabolical as H. H. Holmes. This house has lots of secret passages and as we know, many murders were committed herein."

Baker hadn't released her arm. "Who hung out here? I mean...was he friends with the cleverest minds of the day? The wall slid open? Dropped back?"

"I'm sure he bought the best minds of the day to build this place. You ever play that '90's game *Myst*? The guy who wrote the code for it created a house with 1700 feet of secret passageways."

Baker scanned the dark recesses open before them. "I know of the game. I don't think it plays on any platforms now in use. I wonder if this was all done with magnets. I've seen that before. Maybe the piano rests atop a trigger magnet and when touched or moved, it opens the wall."

"Sure. Did it go up? Where is it? Things just do not disappear."

Baker sighed. "The wall is still here. It has to be." He stood his ground and tugged on Sanz's arm. "Let's explore, shall we?"

"In the ripple room? It's terribly dark. And I have some concerns about the wall not being properly closed the last time someone used it. Hell, Baker. Only me and Mom live here."

Baker reached into his sporran and withdrew a set of housekeys. "I have a little flashlight on my key chain. Let's, shall we?" He flicked on his tiny flashlight but put it away and chose to use his cell.

"I vote no." Sanz shook her head. "No."

Baker pulled her by the arm beyond the vanished wall of canvas and silk trim and cigar smoke stains. One step beyond the barrier between smoking room and unknown darkness, Baker turned and shone his little light against the frame of where the wall had been. "Well, look at this, would ya? It's a backdrop that rises. Like in theaters. How freaking clever."

Sanz clung to his arm. "No difference to the sheer terror I feel."

"I've known you for four or five hours now—and we've already lived through worse than a dark room. I count spirit possession and the knowledge that Albert was not only a perv, but a murderer, as higher on the terror scale than a dark room. Even one that adjoins a well-lit room. It's like no light reflects into this place." Baker paused. 'Yeah. That kind of creeps me out a bit." He shone his light to the right, then left, trying to gauge the size of the room.

"I do not know what this place is. It's not listed. Room behind fake wall. Nope. Not there." Sanz bravely released Baker's arm and followed the light trail to a sheet-draped piece of furniture. She carefully lifted an edge. "Chair."

"Pull the cloth off. There's something familiar about it."

"Your memory, or hers?" Sanz asked, carefully decloaking the chair so as not to stir any more dust than they already had.

"Hers. Definitely, hers." Baker approached the uncovered chair. He shone the light upon it, illuminating it section by section.

"Oddly shaped. A U-shaped seat," Sanz said.

"Thick arms with groove for fingers to clutch. Thin back so others can assist. It's a birthing chair, Sanz—complete with religious icon for the mother to beat her head against while praying for death while squeezing out the spawn."

Sanz grimaced. "Albert...you sick..." She stopped herself from using a heavy curse word. "Shine your light along the wall. I want to see if there is a switch or pull cord or something that can shine more light upon this rather macabre room."

Baker crisscrossed the wall closest the chair. "Ah. Lantern."

"Childbirth by lantern. In the back of a men's smoking room with a fake wall. I wonder if they watched. Maybe placed bets on how long it took to deliver the baby, or if it was male or female." Sanz took up the lantern and shook it. "There's oil in the base." She lifted the glass globe. "And the wick is intact."

Baker deflected the light into his sporran. "I have matches." He withdrew a pack of matches bearing the name of Beacon Shores' only Chinese restaurant. He passed his keys to Sanz and struck a match. It popped and sparked, then settled into a blue flame. He lit the wick. It, too, popped and sparked and sputtered, but eventually succumbed to the kiss of fire. He fit the globe into place and lifted it by the carrying handle.

He and Sanz began uncovering other pieces.

An exam table, completed with leather straps to hold the patient in place. A head cage. Sanz slipped it over her head. "Wicked." She removed it quickly. "And heavy. Really heavy. Maybe Albert was afraid of being bitten."

Baker gulped. "Check this out. It's a tray of syringes too large to be for blood draws. And that vial is labeled mercury. Those are some nasty looking needles. And blunt. That is how they used to treat syphilis in men. By an injection of mercury right up the old peen hole."

"Those poor girls. And the babies. Venereal disease. Jesus Christ. Actually, that could explain some of his crazy. I read once it makes Swiss cheese of brain tissue." Sanz lifted a dust-riddled sheet from a long flat object. "It's a cage. Like a cage where you lay down."

"That is an Utica Crib." Baker pushed the tray of syringes aside and shivered.

"How the heck do you know the proper name for an implement of torture?" Sanz asked.

"She knows. She remembers."

"Creeptastic. This is the last place her spirit should dwell. What's next. An Iron Maiden? Thumb screws?"

The lantern cast an eerie glow against the three walls. Any number of items hung off hooks. Some simple and innocent looking. A pair of pliers. A fire iron. Sanz opened an armoire. "It's linens. Hospital gowns. Some of this is more modern looking. That does not bode well that current era items are in this room. Folded and put away, yet. Oh! Baker. Found it. Light pull. It's next to the armoire."

"Are we sure we want to see the entirety of this room?" Baker asked. "There is something seriously wrong here. It deflects light. I think unspeakable horrors happened within these walls."

"Yes, childbirth by very young Chinese mine workers, injections to cure venereal disease—probably into one of the sick f's who impregnated her, and let's not forget their idea of a waiting room. A cage." Sanz pulled the cord. Two bare lightbulbs flickered on. "Hmmm...again, electricity was an afterthought. Look at the old knob and tube electrical and cotton wire. Jeez. Mother is not going to be happy about this." She turned and pointed at the birthing chair, Utica Crib, and torturous looking devices lining the walls. "Or any of this."

Baker extinguished the oil lamp. "Wait a minute. I want to look into this chamber from the smoking room." He walked into their initial room and stepped up onto a walnut end table. "Holy crap. It's a medical theatre. From this room you can view everything in the comfort of a Chesterfield chair with your whiskey. Was the birth of the product of rape so fascinating it needed an audience? What did he do to those girls?"

Sanz shivered. "Let's not assume it had any legitimate purpose. There's no separate entrance—at least not one that is visible. The smoking room has a secret entrance. It has a heavy canvas wall so cleverly constructed that at first glance—and second glance—it appears to be solid. The mechanism to hoist the *trompe l'oeil* wall was not an afterthought. It is built into the floor, with the pianoforte being the trigger. It is ingenious. This room is framed like a stage. A stage for what production? Who were the performers and who directed? Incidentally, this all the séance stuff is in that oak armoire by sideboard and that non-descript little door next to it. I've not crossed that threshold yet. I peeked, made the sign of the cross and backed away slowly. The wall cabinet is labeled for the whiskey and cigars. And as for the smell...well, I'm sorry to say that there are a number of folded cotton cloths for use. To clean up the spunk."

"Albert was crazy, my friend. Crazy, crazy, crazy. I bet he and his buddies bet on everything from how long it took a worker to cry out, to like you said, whether it was a boy or girl birthed." Baker stopped and leaned forward, squinting.

"What are you doing?" Sanz asked.

"The floor—the floor in the secret room. It has markings. Characters."

Sanz knelt and ran her fingertips across the floor. "It feels waxy."

"You can't see it from there, can you?" Baker asked.

"No."

"Sanz—I can read it. It's in English. It is a shadow under layers of floor wax. Someone left us a message." He paused. "Well, maybe not us." He paused again. "No, it's for us."

Sanz knelt to examine the floor. "I see nothing."

"No, you've got to be higher, and at an angle."

She moved quickly to Baker's perch, climbing atop the table with him.

Perched closely, holding each other for stability, they read the words together.

"Today I die. Today I go to my ancestors. May my shame not push them away. It is a heavy burden I carry across the mountains of death. But I think it is better to die, than to see another child of my body done in. I am a goner. I feel it. The Boss will snuff San Lin's light now. He comes. I die. Ancestors, I put my spirit to you for safe-keeping until I my bones are buried with you. San Lin. 1886."

Baker and Sanz stared at the words etched below layers of wax. They spoke simultaneously. "We need to find her bones."

CHAPTER FIVE

More determined than freaked out, they exited the medical suite, brought down the fabulous canvas wall and ate their lukewarm pizza silently.

Baker broke the stillness. "Has anyone actually confirmed that San Lin died in the shaft cave-in of 1886? That which occurred somewhere far under the grounds of this house? What if it was in a different shaft than the one that connects to your sub-basement?"

Sanz looked up from her phone. "She wasn't important enough for someone to have recorded her death. No penis. If you get my drift. No offense intended."

"Females had little to no value to Albert. Right."

"Family lore says she died on December 12, 1886." Sanz sighed and closed her eyes.

"You all right?" Baker asked.

"I am enhancing my calm. I may be a genius, but this stuff is enough to push me over the edge into a flail. My flails aren't pretty. Mother keeps Lorazepam on hand for those rare instances when I become so overwhelmed, I can't see straight. My neuro-spiciness is high intelligence. All my little synapses don't fire at the same time—until they do."

"Guess I'd better read up," Baker replied.

Sanz nodded as she pulled the crust of her slice. She swallowed. "Historical records, which may or may not be accurate, allude to San Lin's death and the death of several other Chinese slaves by drowning in a mine shaft that collapsed allowing sea water to envelope them. She's mentioned by name because she was Albert's wife. Legally."

"Right. But which mine shaft, exactly. Local legend says it's the one under this house."

"I have no idea how far we can safely go. The elevator will take us to the root cellar, which is what you might call a sub-basement. I've not investigated further. Though there is an old door across from the lift that may lead down into the vestibule of the mines, and places beyond. Mother will not be amused if we go down there."

"Let's go down there," Baker said.

"This alleviation of extreme boredom is getting the best of me. We'll need flashlights—maybe the ones on our phones will be enough. But Lord help us if we need keys."

"We have the key to the witch's cap. Maybe it serves more than one purpose." Baker tugged on her arm.

"If the shaft is sealed by rebar and concrete how do we pass that blockade?" Sanz checked the flashlight on her phone.

"I suppose dynamite is out." Baker paused. "If the concrete is a hundred years old, we can probably knock it in with our feet."

"Let's find out."

Through the secret door in the wall, leaving the pizza and cans behind, they zipped into the hallway. "The lift is east wing territory. Let me warn you—that is one dank, dusty place. We have to go passed the evil clown, too."

"No wonder your mom doesn't like the east wing."

Sanz nodded. "Mother hates the east wing and we are both entirely creeped out by the circus clown themed toybox that is so out of place for this house that it must be a haunted item. I think there's a TV show about that stuff. I should call them."

Baker and Sanz crept down the hallway, Baker again fascinated by the various and sundry objects of kitsch and true art. "You could have the yard sale to end all yard sales. I mean...who wouldn't want to buy a bronze weasel statue from a bonafide haunted house? I get goosebumps just thinking about it."

"I'll let you have first stab if we are ever lucky enough to unload some of this stuff." Sanz paused before a plastic tarp taped to an archway. "This is the east wing."

"Through the plastic instead of the looking glass?"

Sanz carefully lifted the right edge of the tape and slipped through the barrier. Baker followed. "Well, Mother has at least, thought about the east wing. This is new." She tapped a bucket filled with cleaning supplies with her foot. "I have no idea how long this section of the house has gone unused. I suppose we could do scientific measurement using the thickness of the dust."

Baker ran his index finger along an exposed edge of furniture. The dust pushed forward like a bulldozer in dirt. "It's fairly bright in here." He looked up. "Ah, skylights, only partially obstructed by red...red something. Cellophane?"

"Old shit needs to get pulled down. I know there are

lights here somewhere, but I'm not sure we need to illuminate the decay any more than it is now. This room is the ballroom. Yes, ballroom as in cotillions, masquerades, soirées, and fêtes. There is a dumbwaiter that still works—and I'd love to ride it sometime—that leads to the main kitchen. Here is a small stage for musicians, a once undoubtedly fully stocked bar, and off to the side, the ladies sitting room." She placed the back of her hand against her forehead and acted as though she were swooning. "It's all too much to bear, Baker. Please, help me to a settee where I might regain my composure."

"Snap out of it, woman. You are far from the weaker sex. I will never understand why men subjugated women with gusto, for so long. Or why they do it now. Sickens me."

"You're a good man, Baker. Oh...I mean... genderfluid..."

"It's all right, Sanz. Being genderfluid means I can explore both my masculine and feminine side and depending upon whom I am with, different aspects of those sides will emerge. I am more manly with you. So, calling me a good man is fine. I will not argue or correct people about personal pronouns. I know who I am. I accept who I am."

Sanz sighed. "You are the most well-adjusted eighteen-year-old I have ever met."

"I do my best. And I'll be nineteen next week." Baker strolled forward across the dusty floor. "Shall we dance?" He held his arms out as if waltzing and turned gracefully. "My dance card is full, but for a girl like you, I'll make up an excuse for my next partner that you just had to dance this waltz or simply die." He used a fake Southern accent.

Sanz giggled and fell into Baker's arms. They moved

to an unheard rhythm, making circles in the dust, surrounded by tiny dirt devils whipped up by their feet. "That band is tricky. Switching the music mid-beat. It's a much slower dance now. A waltz," Baker said. He and Sanz enveloped each other. Her head went to his chest, his hands to the small of her back.

If ever there had been a more perfect moment for them, in their eighteen years of life on earth, they would have been hard-pressed to recall it. They swayed to music only they could hear. Sanz realized they were so close that she could feel her bosom pressed against his rib cage, and the sensation of his hands and long fingers against her backside was magical. She felt his breath against the top of her head and heard the thump of his heart. He smelled good. She was safe. Safe from her own evil ancestors. Safe from the dust and salt, the mystery and what lay below—in the mine shaft.

"Do you play piano? You have great finger extension."

———

Baker liked how she felt in his arms. This was a girl who could accept his true nature—his duality. He could be a man, in all the ways society said he should be a man, yet still be fully in touch with his feminine side and move with the grace of the goddess. Sanz would never be ashamed of him. Never ridicule him. "Heh. My weight trainer said the same thing." He spread his hand out so that his fingertips touched the top of her rearend.

They stopped swaying to the music only they could hear and looked into each other's eyes. Baker broke the stillness between them. "I hadn't expected that."

Sanz nodded. "Me either."

"I don't know what I'm feeling right now. It feels good. It feels right. It is frightening as hell," Baker said. "From zero to ninety in a few moments. I am now very interested in exploring a relationship with you, Sanz."

"I suppose what we feel is normal. Aren't most kids our age engaged in the customary mating rituals that precede adulthood?" Sanz sighed. "You know what this means, don't you?"

"That we will wear matching corsages to homecoming? It's a pretty big deal at the college."

She patted Baker's chest. "We'd better pause this love fest up before we break our vow of chastity." She laughed nervously and took a step back. Sanz tripped over a chair leg and yelped as she hit the floor. She leapt up as quickly as she had fallen. "I meant to do that. Really. Comic relief."

"Are you all right? Oh, Sanz. Your arm is bleeding." Baker reached into one of the pockets of his utilikilt and withdrew a tissue. He passed it to Sanz. "Your arm is going to have one heck of a bruise."

"It's okay. I kind of have this reduced sensitivity to pain. I honestly wouldn't have noticed the scrape until the blood trickled off my hand. Don't worry, Baker."

"You'd be great to fake out someone like Jigsaw. You know...from the *Saw* movies. Pain is half his game."

"I'm not supposed to watch those kinds of movies. Mother thinks I'm too smart and might blow a gasket and start reenacting scenes. That said, I've seen them all and I could build way better traps."

"Remind me not to get on your bad side."

Sanz smiled. "I doubt that will ever happen. Now, I'm fine. Let's find that stupid lift."

She wanted to hold his hand. Chills ran up her spine

as the back of their hands brushed together as they slipped between decorative columns pushed together like wallflowers at a dance.

The airspace between them had become palpable. Thicker than the dust that covered—well—everything in the ballroom. The remains of the afternoon sun shone through the red-filtered skylights making pockets of light alive with the floating particles.

"Ah, there. Second star to the right and on until morning. Or just passed the hell o' a clown toybox, which frighteningly enough, is chained and padlocked shut. The wrought iron elevator with cage and ornate lever once operated by one of Albert's paid or captive servants. I don't know which."

Baker paused at the toybox. The chains around it were ancient and thick and the lock, heavy. "That is one seriously scary box. Three-inch chains and an old railroad lock." He took the turret key from Sanz and passed it into the keyhole. It fit. "Bloody hell. This key could unlock certain doom." He removed it quickly. "Can we pass on opening it for now? The energy between the lock and key is tangible and seriously uncomfortable. Do you know how to operate the elevator?"

Sanz laughed. "I'm not touching that box. The elevator is old school easy. Slide the lever down to go down and pull it up quickly at the floor you'd like disembark. Except you never know exactly which way the lift is going to move. It's quite like the great glass elevator in the Willy Wonka books. It moves just as erratically."

"Sounds fun. I can't wait."

Sanz went ahead of Baker and tried to pull open the cage. Age and disuse, again her nemesis to exploration, thwarted her. "Baker? Not to sound sexist or needy, but could you use those upper arm muscles of yours to get this thing open?"

He chuckled. "Step aside. I'll give it a try." He worked up a bit of a sweat, but two great pulls later he had opened the cage. They stepped inside. He closed it—this time it slid easily. He read the stops on the lever aloud. "Attic. Ballroom. Hearth room. Scullery. Basement. Below." Someone had scratched off the words sub-basement, but they were still legible. "Does it matter which one we choose?"

Sanz shook her head. "Not really. It has a mind of its own. Go ahead and move the lever to *below*. Let's see what happens."

Baker wrapped his long fingers around the filigree brass lever and slowly moved it to the lowest destination. The antique elevator sputtered and popped, then lurched up hard. He lost his footing and fell against Sanz. They hit the deck, her hands held his upper arms and her chest and shoulders held the bulk of his weight.

She laughed. "Forgot to mention that it starts up with a bang."

Baker sighed and dropped to his knees. "Jeez. Thanks for the crash pad." He wrapped his arms around her waist and hugged her, his head to her chest.

A hot flush ran through her from toes to forehead. She hesitantly slid her arms around him. The lift hummed and moved down, through the dark shaft. Pitch black between floors, it was both creepy and titillating.

Baker slowly stood and pressed against her, pinning her to the back of the lift. Her arms were around his neck and his arms held her waist tightly. That's when their lips met. In the blackness.

It wasn't her first kiss.

It was obviously not his.

She allowed herself to relax a bit and enjoy the sweet pressure of pressing bodies and warm, wet mouths.

Baker broke the embrace. "I'm sorry. It just seemed like the right time. Darkness can hide a multitude of sins."

Sanz giggled. "Or a fine collection of them."

The elevator came to a halt with a loud thud and sound of creaking cables.

"Is this it?" Baker asked.

"Yep. First try. Must be our lucky day."

"Lights?"

"Cell phones."

Baker stepped out of the lift and flicked on his cell phone flashlight. Better than nothing. "What is that smell, Sanz?" he asked.

"Dead things, Baker. Dead things. This anti-chamber is carved out of solid rock. We are a good twelve feet under the mansion. Here there be monsters. If memory serves, the way to the shaft is straight ahead and down. It's an incline. Very gradual. And I know this only from reading one of the ledgers. Sometimes Albert stored things down here. Like wine. And gun powder."

"Are there any guns here?" Baker asked.

"Don't know. I've never explored this smelly catacomb before other than to get a whiff when the elevator took me here. Several times, I might add. That's why Mom made it off limits. From what I read, there is a literal hole in the bedrock that leads to into the mine shaft."

"The one that flooded?"

"Unknown. I guess if we find a cap of iron and concrete, the answer is yes."

Baker stopped. He shone the light on his face. "Do you feel the tingle in the air?"

Sanz raised her light to her face. "No."

"Shhhh...hold your breath for a second and let the thick air of this place envelope you. I swear, we are not alone."

"Probably not, Baker. You aren't going to channel San Lin again, are you?"

"Admittedly, I am very sensitive to these things, but I believe we are surrounded by very powerful memories. And I feel her presence very strongly. I could allow her spirit to speak through me."

Sanz took his hand. "If you speak for San Lin, do I have to relive Albert's drama?"

Baker held out his phone as far as it could go ahead of him. "I think we should both keep the spirit doors closed until we are out of this place."

"Word."

They moved ahead slowly, staying within the confines of the glow of their cell lights. Her hand in his left, clasped firmly, providing some semblance of safety in the unknown dark of the shaft.

Baker shone his light aloft. "This shaft is at least seven feet high. I'm six four and I can reach the grimy, sooty ceiling with my hand."

"Let's not applaud the builders yet. I'm sure something untoward is about to occur. Moving into this place has been one circus after another. And the problem with that is, it really is my circus and they are my monkeys." Sanz paused. "It is a wonder I haven't had a complete meltdown yet."

"Not on my watch, friend." Baker squeezed her hand.

"The end of this tunnel must be just ahead. We've

gone at least twelve feet and if memory serves, the shaft wasn't more than fifteen feet from the lift. In fact, I know it. Eidetic memory."

"Bingo," Baker replied. He waved his phone so that the light illuminated the back wall and metal ladder. And concrete cap.

"Well, local legend rings true. The shaft is sealed." Sanz stomped her foot against the century-old concrete slab. It moved slightly from the weight and pressure. "Woah. It isn't stable. Don't step on this, Baker."

"I so want to step on it, Sanz. I want to crush it with the heels of my Doc Martins, climb down that ladder and see what there is to see."

"I'm not sure I want to see the remains of my great-great-great-great grandmother."

"If we find her bones, you will literally pull the rubber mask off the bad guy just like in Scooby Doo. I'm sorry he's related to you."

Sanz sighed. "I hope his brand of crazy doesn't run in the family."

"I think we should go for it. Let's put her to rest. Once that happens, maybe everything else will fall into place. Can we ship bones to China where her ancestors are buried?" Baker reached for the ladder and gave it a hard pull. It was secured to the shaft wall. He leaped up and caught the first wrung with his foot. He held on to the ladder and stomped his other foot on the crumbling concrete seal. A small piece fractured off as if he'd used a cheese slicer. He stomped again. And again. With each impact the seal cracked further. "Since her daughters are buried here, so-to-speak, probably in a mine shaft somewhere, maybe her ancestors will accept this place as a burial ground. Your mom won't mind if we do a little gardening, right?"

Sanz stayed back, her phone's light shining upon the slab. "I was jazzed to find her bones a couple hours ago. In theory, it was an awesome idea. In practice, it's leaving me cold." She watched with interest as Baker turned to get a better aim using his heel. He smashed down with all high might. His kilt flew up. For a moment Sanz wished she had a better light. She chastised herself for even considering such a thing. *This is not a time to get excited over the muscular thighs of the gender non-specific boy next door.* "Wow, Baker. You just knocked a hole in hundred-year-old concrete without breaking a nail. Impressive."

He laughed. "Oh, gods...it smells bad. Whatever has been buried here is beyond rotted."

The odor struck Sanz and she gagged. "That is nasty. Foul air. Stagnant water. Dead things."

"All of the above." Baker shone his light down the hole. "The ladder is intact. It goes down to a platform. A very old platform. Although I fight against stereotypical gender roles...ladies first?"

"I guess I am the granddaughter of the ghost of Christmas past, or whatever. Yes. I'll go first." Sanz tucked away her cell phone and took hold of the ladder. "Keep that light on, Baker." She cringed at the feel of the cold metal against her hands. She wanted to vomit. Rung by rung, slow and careful she climbed down about seven feet to the wood and iron platform. "You're turn," she called up to Baker.

"Don't look up my kilt," Baker said as he climbed down into the dark hole.

She did, once again damning the lack of light.

Lit only by their cell phones, they surveyed the vestibule.

"That pile of rocks and debris just ahead of us—it must be the opening to the mine shaft," Sanz said. She palmed a small stone and set it aside. "Come on. Let's find out what's on the other side of it."

Baker moved closer and moved his phone from floor to ceiling all the way around the rocky barrier. "This entrance is made of iron reinforced lumber. I'll hazard to guess that removing rocks will not cause a cave in." He paused and held out his hand to stop Sanz's movement. "Shhhh. Stop. I hear water. Moving water."

Sanz froze. "Yes. Just beyond this mine entrance. I hear it. I don't recall there being running water under the house. A subterranean stream, maybe?"

"It could be a channel to the bay. Water rushes in and out with the tide. We learned of such things in local history. I never thought much of it until now. My science teacher back in 7th grade told me that other mine shafts filled up with all sorts of debris from tidal pull. Lawn chairs, crates from Japan. All kinds of weird shit."

Sanz passed Baker a rock. The gold band on her ring finger tingled. "I wonder if her bones will still be there. If this is even the right place." Baker had not yet taken the fist-sized stone. "Yo, Baker. Take this sucker." She turned to face her friend. Even in the half-light of their cell phones, she could see the difference in him. Felt the difference in him. "Who's riding shotgun now?"

Baker's right hand flew out and struck Sanz across the cheekbone. She stumbled backward but didn't fall.

"Damn. Albert." Sanz backed away.

Baker, his face swollen and red, screamed, "You should not meddle in my affairs. Damned do-gooder

Catholics. Get off my property. Get off now or I will release my dogs—and you have heard of what they can do, no doubt."

Sanz stood her ground. "Wake up, Baker. Now would be a good time to have both feet in this reality." Baker was lost to the possession. *He must not be able to hear me. However, Albert can.*

The tirade continued. "My workers are far from abused. They are paid a decent wage and are given food and shelter. I don't know where this rumor started that my men take indecent liberties and otherwise abuse the girls. I need workers of smallish size. They fit comfortably in the carts. Why, they sit all day. How hard could that work be? They are quick and can sort the coal with precision. Separating by size is important a job as any in my mines."

Sanz rubbed her cheek and moved her jaw side-to-side. *Damn. This hurts. Do I play along? Do I book it out of here?* She chose to continue moving rocks to clear the opening. Ignore the crazy. She worked silently, the sound of her hands moving fist-sized stones and Baker's uneven, heavy breaths, the only sound in the darkness. He had turned off his cell phone—or it had died. Only her cell, resting on a larger stone she couldn't move alone gave off light. *I don't know much about spirit possession, but Baker should have some kind of guards up to prevent sneak attacks. If we get out of this, I am so going to talk to him about such things. Am I going to get out of this? He hasn't moved. If I turn, what am I going to see?* Several minutes had passed. She had made a dent in the barrier. Sanz brushed off her hands and turned. Baker was in the shadows. The whites of his eyes glowed. "Baker?"

"Granddaughter, have you come to make offerings to

the ancestors?" Baker's voice no longer had the harsh rasp and force of Albert Whitmore.

"Okay. Sure," Sanz replied. "San Lin?"

"Yes, granddaughter. It is I."

"Is Baker okay?" Sanz reached for her phone and slowly lifted the light to shine on Baker's face.

"He is here. Asleep." Baker's lips continued to move, though it was not his voice that emanated. "I have held my breath for over a hundred years. There is a word I would speak so that my ancestors and descendants can exact revenge. I will speak the foul, stinging word upon burial of my bones and see the end of his empire. Such power lay in words, granddaughter."

"Are you here? Your remains. Beyond here? Where are your feet?" Sanz motioned to the wall of rock she had been clearing.

"No longer."

"Where can I find you?"

"He wanted me close. He wanted to control me in death as he had in life. As he defiled me in life, he defiles me in death. As he tortured me in life, he tortures me in death. I am with him now. Our bodies are intertwined in a lewd position. His corruption is vast."

Sanz took a deep breath and calmed her racing heart. This situation was at the far end of her tolerance spectrum. Melt down imminent. The high level of intelligence within her fought against the rising tide of panic. Three deep breaths. Then it dawned on her. "Are you buried with Albert?" She paused, watching carefully as Baker/San Lin nodded. *That's not here. Not in Beacon Shores. It's on an island.* She wracked her brain trying to remember the name. *San Juan Island.*

Baker's continence changed as smoothly as a rolling

wave against the shore. "You gutter snipe! You cheating whore! What have you done with it? You know it is not to be touched. I will see you swing for this!"

Oh shit. Sanz felt her skin prickle. Extra-large goose bumps. From the base of her skull a burgeoning headache became an unbearable pressure and when she opened her mouth to cry out, it was not her voice that burst forth. San Lin had emerged. "Someday the law will find your ledger and know the truth about what you have done to us, Albert Whitmore. When our bodies fall into dust and your dynasty is rotted and decrepit, your words will be read by those who will enact change. The children of my body will not be your slaves. They will rise up and take back that which you have stolen."

"I should have never taught you English, you little snipe. You almost sound civilized. Good that you will never look English. Your voice may tempt others into believing you are learned. Your face never shall."

"There is a name for men such as yourself," San Lin replied.

"Yes. God. I am God to you."

"I do not believe in your God. I rely on my ancestors."

"Idolatry. You worship false prophets, not the Creator. I have seen your acts of geomancy and your scrawl of prayers cut into the walls of my house. When your last breath is expelled, it will be my God to whom you cry out."

"I will sing to my ancestors as I die and hold the name of my murderer within the confines of my last breath that they may know your name. Your accursed name."

CHAPTER SIX

Baker awoke first. He hurt everywhere. His mouth and throat burned. All he wanted was water. A long, cold drink. He reached for his phone. Dead. It was then he recalled where he was. The entrance to the pit. The fabled mine shaft wherein the bones of murdered Chinese children lay. But he now knew at least *her* bones were not lost in this dark place. "Sanz? You there?"

She moaned. "What?"

"Are you all right?"

Sanz sat upright. "I've been with it for a little while, just kind of mulling over the whole speaking-for-the-dead thing. I'm not a charismatic, nor am I psychic on any level. Why the heck am I suddenly channeling my late great-great-great-great grandmother? There's a missing ledger. It tells where his grave is—and hers."

Baker coughed. "I need water. Let's get out of here. Is your phone still charged?"

"Using the flashlight drained it. I have like 6% remaining and have the usual bells and whistles of low battery flashing. My head is killing me."

"If I'm not mistaken the intrusive possession we just suffered saved us from digging through this rubble any further. Her bones aren't here." Baker stood and reached out to help Sanz to her feet.

"She's buried with Albert and he is not buried here. He's on San Juan Island. He's buried somewhere. I don't know where. Who would have done that for him? He died in 1966—eighty years after her. Oh, hi...would you please keep this bag of bones for me and stick it in my coffin someday?" She stood, still clutching his hands. The darkness didn't seem so dark. The dank didn't seem so cold. Not when being held by him. By Baker. He wrapped his arms around her and held her closely. She wanted a kiss. She wanted all the kisses. *Oh, my god. I'm acting like a regular teenager. This is so uncool.*

He released her without fulfilling her desires. She considered the butterflies in the pit of her stomach. *Hmmm. So, this is angst.* She followed Baker up the clammy ladder. At the top, just steps away from the elevator, she mustered courage and took Baker by the waist from behind. He turned in her embrace and replied in kind. She slid her arms around his neck and fell into a deep kiss. Their bodies pressed together, she felt a flutter of arousal—and panicked. Not an audible or demonstrable panic, but definitely an internal one.

Baker broke the kiss and smiled. "Are we pushing ahead too quickly?"

Sanz nodded. "I am feeling things. Things I thought would be absent from my life for many years to come."

"Let's go sit in Goliath and figure out our next steps. Between us—and finding San Lin's bones."

Sanz nodded. "And charge our phones. Do you have your cable?"

He patted his sporran. "Always."

They returned carefully, and quietly, to the upper floor. The lift had a stop just off the glass-encased conservatory next to the big kitchen. Mother had left a note on the counter by the large porcelain sink. "Store."

"She is nothing if not succinct, my mother." Sanz tossed the note in the paper recycle bin. Baker reached out to hold her hand as they meandered through the mansion to the library entrance. The double doors were closed. "Mother hath seen the chip off the old veneer. Damn. Good thing you are here. She would have lit into me. Not that she's volatile—it has to do with the lawyers and their nosey noses."

"We got this, Sanz."

They opened the library and strolled inside. They pulled up chairs at a massive, heavy dark wood table. Their hands outstretched and clutched as they spoke about the bones, the spirits, the mystery. They set their phones up to charge.

"How gross that she's interred with him."

"I wonder where his final resting place is."

"On San Juan Island. It could be anywhere. I've never made the trip." Sanz rubbed her cheek that had taken the blow.

"I'm sorry about that," Baker said. "The bitch slap."

"I'll be fine. If it bruises makeup can cover it. Or I can tell Mom I stumbled and tripped—that she will believe. We need to look up how to protect ourselves from possession. There must be a book about that in here somewhere."

"Or google it. It's called warding."

"Warding. All right. We need to ward ourselves before

—before we go bone hunting. We will get to take a ferry. I've never been on a ferry."

"The salt."

"What?"

"Albert was using the salt to ward himself from the spirits of the people he killed. Salt repels. He was afraid."

Sanz laughed. "Ya think? So am I!"

"Salt is a good ward, but we need something stronger if we're to, and I mean this literally, dig up his grave and re-bury San Lin's bones."

"Baker, how do we tell whose bones are whose?"

"I don't know. But my gut tells me we'll be able to discern without issue."

Sanz sighed and rummaged around a file drawer. "We have no family cemetery or mausoleum. Especially not on an island. At least not that we know of. So...where would a 106-year-old pervert have himself interred?"

"Did he have a right-hand man? Someone he trusted to handle his affairs?"

"The fire boss, I suppose. But I don't think Albert would have mixed folks from the mine with the upper-crust men who more than likely doted on his every wish. In 1966, I'm sure he had a gentleman's gentleman, a maid, a nurse, a whipping boy. He must have left instructions with someone." She paused. "The man kept detailed records. His caregivers must be listed. I know his internment is not listed in his will. I've read it. It could be in the legal documents in his ledgers. Now that I understand all the little bird notations are children, the ledgers are the stuff of nightmares. He was a meticulous old scab and even on his deathbed I'm sure his inventory was up to date." Sanz rose from the table and pointed at a low, free-standing bookcase hear the porthole windows. "The sum of Albie's life is there. And the missing ledger...we find that and it's the golden ticket."

"His fine collection of sins memorialized in oversized ledger books. Twisted."

"So as we let our fingers do the walking, are we going to talk about that kiss?" Sanz asked, knowing her yellow pages reference might be too obscure for Baker.

Baker placed his palms on the table and looked up slowly. "Do you want to hang out with a non-binary gender fluid human? Maybe explore companionship in a safe and non-threatening way that will fill us with joy and not teenaged angst?"

"Well, since you put it that way, yes. You do not trigger me, Baker. Some people just send me over the edge. I'm sure Albert would have."

"Albert would have had you, relative or not, working the mines before you were out of pull-ups. All children got from this place was pain from the toybox. Not love. Not shelter."

"Toybox. Creepy. I am perseverating. I hate clowns."

"As do I." Baker reached across the table and held her hand for a moment. "So, show me the legal files."

"I'm getting overwhelmed. We need to read the ledgers, find a way to ward ourselves against the memories of this house and..."

"What can I do to help you, Sanz?"

"Let's have tea."

Baker laughed. "Tea?"

"Yes. Mom gives me a calming tea and has taught me some deep breathing techniques to help me focus."

"Tea, it is." He walked around the large table and held out his hand.

———

Sanz closed her eyes for a moment as the physical sensation that shook her at the sight of the swish of his kilt made her heady. He was wearing briefs under it. He wasn't being traditional in that sense. *But I liked what I saw. Black underwear. Jesus Christ. I do not want to go through this relationship crap.* She took his hand and let her gaze trail up his arms to his guns. Big muscles. Tight t-shirt. Kilt. Eyeliner and pink-tipped hair. *This guy is hot.* Her hand in his as they strolled to the kitchen seemed authentic and as if nothing that had occurred that day mattered. *This is not okay. It all matters. I cannot lose myself this way. I need to stay poised on the razor's edge. To help San Lin. To change my freaking family karma.* She wanted to press herself against him, feel his body heat. *Damn it, I want to kiss him again. I want to kiss him longer and deeper. What is the matter with me? What's wrong with him? We professed wanting nothing to do with the dating scene and here we are just about mashing on a sofa. Brain overload.*

She plugged in the electric kettle and pulled out a nice herbal tea from the drawer. "Seriously, this will help. Taking the time for a cup of tea does wonders."

Baker straddled a chair, using the chairback as an armrest. "Whatever you need. I like tea. While we're waiting, can I go explore the salt cupboard?"

"Seriously...there's nothing in there but salt. Lots and lots of salt."

"I know." He rose and turned on his cell light. "I found that Tudor Rose box in here. Maybe I'll find a clue."

"We are sounding more and more like an episode of Scooby Doo."

"We're going to pull the rubber mask off the bad guy, Sanz. Just wait and see."

"Right now getting this monkey off my back will be enough. I feel as though a hundred sets of eyes are gazing upon. Judging me. No...*urging* me."

"To solve this mystery?"

She approached Baker in the salt room and pressed herself against him, arms around his neck and one leg slid between his. She kissed him with all the passion she could muster. Lips parted. Tongues touching. Thankfully, he responded in kind. And then some. Baker turned her and put his full weight into pressing her against the wall, not breaking the embrace.

It was a desperate dance of hands and mouths, hips urging and bodies aching for a deep breath.

Baker broke away without taking his weight off her. "I know what to do here—but I don't want to ruin what we already have by going at things too soon. Too hard. I haven't felt this kind of passion for anyone before."

Sanz exhaled onto his throat. "Yes."

"I've never gone all the way—but I've been around the block. And Sanz...I'm demisexual. You figured that out, right? Hearts, not parts."

"If reason and control didn't ground me so thoroughly, I would reach under your kilt."

"You peeked on the ladder, didn't you?"

She giggled. "Oh yes."

"When we're ready...when we are not literally in the company of your tortured ancestors' souls, we can do what we want. And Sanz, I want you. When we're truly ready."

"Someday."

"Someday." Baker led another kiss and smoothed his

hand down her arms and briefly brushed his fingertips across her chest.

Sanz felt an incredible flood of arousal course through her body. "We need to stop, or I won't be able to." She internally chastised herself for stopping as the feeling of his bulge from under his kilt was insanely enticing as it pressed against her. "I think what we are experiencing is a part of this whole ghostly—and ghastly—field trip into the memories of this place. There's more to San Lin's story than what we've been shown. I know it."

"Not psychic, huh? But I agree with you. Something in the wake of horrors Albert created, there is deep affection wafting about and I for one, have been captured by that tide. I want you to know that above all things, I respect you. Let's cherish our friendship and help you conquer the weirdness that is this house and your DNA."

"I'll let you help. I can't do this alone."

"Hey...what's this?" He reached onto a high shelf and pulled away an old postcard.

"A creepy clown picture. A circus nightmare. How old is it?"

"This is older than dirt. I can't make out the writing on it. Maybe in more light."

"Let's get our tea and take this potential clue or nightmare out to the veranda. Or we could sip in the greenhouse."

"I wondered if that thing was structurally sound."

"It's pretty cool. I mean...this house is dark. Just look at the curtains upstairs. The greenhouse is bright. There are screens on the windows and some of them are broken, but with a little work, it will be glorious. Like a lanai, only larger, older, and overlooking everything."

"Two stories, too. East wing."

"I assume it illuminates the horrors of that end of the house. It is god-awful dirty."

"Let's drink our calming tea, which frankly, I want quite desperately."

"Sugar? Honey?"

"Honey, please."

Sanz made tea and put the pot and two cups, a couple honey straws and napkins on a tray. Baker followed her to the conservatory.

"Jesus Christ. This place is huge."

"Bigger than it looks from the outside, huh? It is the only place in the house I do not feel creeped out. I think the mint green décor mixed with ancient potting soil, the remains of plants past and the light make it...nicer. Of course, it is scary as hell at night."

Baker tilted his head back and looked straight up. "This must have been a marvel."

"The east wing ballroom connects to that landing up there. Can you image? If Albie had been human, there would have been dances. Not death."

Baker removed a clear plastic tarp from a settee and sat. He added honey to his cup then poured the tea for them both. "So...let's shed some light on this grotesque antique postcard." He held it out, catching the light. "There's a date printed on the card, Sanz. 1965."

"The year before he died."

"Sick old fool. 1965 and a clown. But it's not his handwriting. It's in the same hand as parts of his grimoire."

"Maybe he was making amends."

Baker took a sip of his tea. "How so?"

"He was suffering from dementia by 1965. Hooked up to machines. Skin and bones. Unless he was a total psychopath, he may have been remorseful."

"He was a total psychopath."

"But the clown on the card is similar to the toybox. I am truly disinterested in opening that ugly chest and releasing whatever is locked within. What if San Lin wrote it from beyond the grave? I mean...she wasn't buried. She was bagged up and left to decay until he died. Spirit writing."

Baker sipped his tea silently, then shuddered. "Sanz?"

"Yes?"

"It's going to happen again."

Sanz immediately thought about their grope in the salt closet but knew better. "Who?"

Baker set his cup down and craned his neck backward until he faced the vault of the ceiling. His hands went rigid. "You are far too unwomanly. You should go home and tend to your surviving children."

Albert. Crap. "They are fine." *Do I play along?*

"She is mine and always will be. Every part of her. From her body to her soul, she is mine."

"You can't own another person," Sanz replied, realizing that ownership of a human had been a thing—in the past.

"I won't sell her."

That's odd. "I'm not asking to buy her."

"If you want to use her spiritual gifts, I'll invite you to a séance. She is quite adept. But she is mine."

"Who am I to you?" she asked.

"The wife of my foreman, of course. Your husband should beat you more often, as you are impudent and far too vocal for a woman."

"How much to have San Lin contact the spirit of my late son?" *I can play along.*

"A thousand dollars for an hour—whether or not she makes contact."

"Done." *That's over three-thousand dollars now. Christ, what a monster.*

"I shall speak to your husband about payment. San Lin is in her confinement right now as she recently birthed me another son. It will be a month, at least." Baker tilted his head forward and gazed hard at Sanz.

She held her breath.

Baker fell out of the chair.

"Shit! Baker!" Sanz rallied to his side, helping him recline on the settee. "Are you all right?"

"Gods, I hate that man. He makes me feel dirty. I know things about him that are far better left undiscovered. He was a vile, deceitful, pompous asshole."

"Yes. Of this I am aware." She sat on the edge of the mint green old-fashioned sofa and placed her hand protectively on Baker's hip. "How do we stop him from interfering while we work to put San Lin to rest?"

Baker placed a hand atop hers. "I don't know." He unhooked the brass latch on his sporran. "Let's pull cards."

"Cards?"

"My tarot deck."

"I don't know from tarot, Baker."

"I can guide us."

Sanz squeezed his hand. "I said I wanted a reading today."

Baker sat up right. Sanz felt warmth emanating from him. "My, it's cozy in here."

He laughed. "I feel it, too."

"Are we in heat?"

"I promise not to behave like an alley cat." He shuffled

his deck and fanned the cards out on the little table next to the tea tray. He drew three cards and flipped them face up. "All right. The Hermit. The Ace of Wands. And the Empress."

"Means what?" Sanz picked up a card and studied it intently.

"That we are on a journey to discover something marvelous—and we need to do some self-care in the process."

"Ward ourselves, yes. Finish our tea. Go back to Goliath—which seems the safest place right now.

Baker put his cards away. "There are so many meta-physical books in there. I might have some juice now, too. It's been a good thirty minutes. Gods bless the internet."

Sanz didn't reply. She stared at Baker while resting her hand on his thigh, enjoying the sensation of his fingertips intertwining with hers. "I wasn't looking for this."

"Me either," he replied. "But I'm going to kiss you again."

"My mother is going to lose her mind. Pretty sure she thinks you're gay."

"I'll take that as a compliment, actually." He pressed his lips to Sanz's and engaged her in a long, deep kiss. *I want to touch her everywhere and...no. Not yet.*

She reached around his broad shoulders and let herself fall back onto the settee, him nearly atop her.

Heaven help my mother, but I am the one who is losing my mind. Dear Gods, kissing him is both exciting and nurturing. I feel safe with him. He is so unlike any other person I've embraced this way. She held him tightly, wanting to melt into him.

He knew he wasn't himself as they entered the library. The pressure on the back of his neck was firm and decisive. Spirit possession. He recognized it. And then he lost himself. His self-control. His barriers came crashing down and the malevolent spirit of Albert Whitmore took over. He crashed them both to the floor and kissed her wildly. But it was no longer Sanz under him. It was her great-great-great-great grandmother. And she was all his. His kiss grew aggressive as he pinned her body under his. Albert had control.

Sanz sensed the change and tried to end the embrace. "Baker…"

He pushed her legs open and ground his hips into her pelvic bone.

"Baker, no. Stop." She hit him with the bag of salt she'd carried in.

He laughed. But it was not his laugh. Not his voice. Not him. "We are wed and it is your duty to see to my pleasure."

"Bloody hell…no!" Sanz fought against Baker's body as Albert pantomimed the rape of San Lin.

Baker raised a hand to strike Sanz, then catapulted off her and onto the floor. He shook uncontrollably, curling into the fetal position. "Sanz, I'm sorry! I'm sorry." Then calling out into dead air, "Albert Whitmore! I rebuke you! You hateful, vile old man. Leave me alone!"

"I knew it wasn't you." She dropped to her knees beside Baker. "I knew it wasn't you. Albert can go to hell."

"He's already there. Help me off the floor." Sanz extended her hands to him. "I would never force you. I wouldn't force anyone. Poor San Lin. What she must have gone through. She fell into hell alive."

"Yes, well...he assaulted her and murdered her. Time to end that nightmare for her and all those that came after."

"The room under the witch's cap...that's where it happened. He beat her, savaged her and chained her until she submitted. And she did submit. She wanted to live. Especially after she had children—even though he sent the boys away and killed the girls. Her ancestors...*your* ancestors are pissed off."

"I bet they are.Do your thing with the salt, Baker. You know...a circle and along the sills and entrance."

He nodded.

"She was clairvoyant, too. He pimped her out for séances. No wonder she learned English so quickly Sanz shook off the sensation of being touched by Albert's presence and rubbed her hands with salt. She used her understanding of the language as a weapon against Albert. I know it. I feel it." He began spreading the salt.

CHAPTER SEVEN

They sat quietly on a small sofa in the library madly searching online for a ward to protect them.

"I honestly don't know where to begin," Sanz said softly. "The toybox? The legal papers? Find the missing ledger?"

"We've seasoned everything liberally with salt. . That's a start. I'd like to not be jumped by either of them while trying to figure things out."

"It's pretty random."

"The way they appear to us? Yes. I have the feeling that you, too, are a medium. A channeler. Otherwise, neither of them could have spoken through you," Baker replied.

"Yeah...Mom has said the same thing. Apparently, I had relatives...the Alberts, actually, who ran an act. But they were real mediums. Mom's grandfather, I think. But her father was an Albert, too. It gets confusing."

"Alberts. Plural?"

"We are all Alberts."

"Someone could just not name their kid thusly."

"I will. If I have a child, it will not be named any of the myriad forms of Albert."

Baker poured salt along the closed pocket doors while Sanz refilled the dozens of little foil ashtrays.

"Get the portholes, okay? I can't reach."

Baker lined the sills with salt. "To keep things out or in? Why insist on salt as a provision in his last will and testament?"

"He was nuts," Sanz replied.

"Or being haunted." Baker paused. "He was definitely being haunted."

Sanz laughed. "So are we. Was this room where he wanted to make his last stand? I mean...there are salt dishes all over the house, but this room is extra spicy."

Baker too her hand. "A spicy room for a neuro-spicy girl." He laughed. "Seriously...what if he was on to something? What is in this room that screams anti-spirit? It could be anything. The strakes. Incantations written in lemon juice on the walls. The salt. Do you have a black light? A UV?"

Sanz squeezed his hand. "There's one in the flat file along with some rocks that fluoresce. Blue Amber, Tugtupite and Yooperlite."

"Can you darken the room?"

Sanz stood and waved at the built-in ship. "There are hooks above the portholes and the curtains are, as all are fabrics in this house, heavy velvet. I pulled them off their runners to get some light in here. To see the dust. To then vacuum the dust."

"Let's put them back. Darken the room and scope it out with the UV. I'm formulating a theory."

"The curtains are folded up in the far cupboard under

the bookcase with all the biology books. Mom flipped out when I took them down. We have to rehang them before the lawyers visit, anyway."

"No alterations."

"None." Sanz pulled the heavy curtains from their hiding place. "Do you think he had a reason—besides eccentricity? And protection from manifestations of his fine collection of sins."

Baker nodded. "Yep. Everything in here might be a ward. Dude was haunted."

"He deserved it. That said, my psyche can't handle any more attacks from the evil grandfather from hell. Let's figure this out."

"Again, Sanz...I'm really sorry. I was—not myself."

"That much was obvious."

A loud rap on the pocket doors alerted Sanz that her mother was home. "I'll go talk to her. I'd prefer she not see the salt lines. I'm just getting her used to the foil ashtrays." She slipped through the doors.

"Hey. Have a successful trip to the grocery store?"

"Yes. Your friend still here?"

Sanz nodded. "All night. We'll camp out in the library. He's into the books. We had some frozen pizza earlier."

"I'm going to put the groceries away. Do you kids think you could haul them in for me? That way I'll have the energy to go clean something."

"Sure, Mom."

"I'm glad you're making friends."

"He's the best." Sanz motioned for Baker to help lift and tote.

The car was parked above the main walkway, close to the conservatory. It was the closest any vehicle could get. It was still a hike. Two trips.

"Hey, Ma! Did you buy salt?" Sanz yelled.

A flying potholder hit her on the back of the head.

Sanz laughed. "My grandmother on my dad's side used to chuck shoes. At least Mom uses something less lethal."

"My parents barely raise their voices above whispers so that the chi of the house isn't disturbed. Mom has little protective grids on every flat surface."

"Why? You don't live in a haunted mansion."

"No, we don't. But I bring it with me, yanno?"

"Is that a tool we can use here? To keep from getting jumped?"

"I don't think a black tourmaline point and clear quartz will help in this case."

"Why black tourmaline?"

"It absorbs negativity."

Sanz continued. "And clear quartz?

"It amplifies intention."

"There are all kinds of rocks and crystals in Goliath. That old flat file...no maps. It's rocks. Lots of rocks."

"We can try." Baker set his bags on the counter to await Sanz's mother. "Huh. She picked up a ferry schedule."

"Fascinating. Perhaps fate."

"I've made the crossing many times. It stops at Orcas and Lopez Islands, then San Juan. I've got a truck, Sanz. We could cross then look for his tomb."

"Sounds good." *But why don't you have a Buick with a large back seat?*

Baker perused the shelves for books with the most promising titles on the spine. He sighed. "As I assumed, all the anti-possession spells are TV-show related. Not helpful."

"Most of these books were written long before *Supernatural*. The writers must have gotten the idea somewhere. You know...that anti-possession tattoo?"

"We just need to close ourselves off to the sheer amount of anguish in this house. It permeates everything. We need to find her bones."

Sanz unfolded the ferry schedule. "The last ferry is at 9 p.m. The next is at 6 a.m. tomorrow. Why don't we take that one. At least it will be in daylight."

"Parental units..." Baker began.

"I'd rather beg forgiveness than ask permission in this case. We're both of age, anyway. My mother doesn't tell me what to do. Most of the time," Sanz said with assurance.

"We don't know where to look. Exactly."

"Let me see that postcard, Baker."

He passed her the faded circus-themed deltiology.

Sanz shook her head. "These faded numbers...it's latitude and longitude." She quickly typed them into her phone. 48.6159° N, 123.1480° W. Afterglow Vista. It's a mausoleum for the McMillin Family. I know that name. He was a purveyor of lime. Made millions. He died in 1936. His family is interred there. *Weird America*, man. It's good reading."

"He wouldn't be buried with the McMillin family."

"No, but he could be buried near Afterglow Vista. There are old graves along the path." Sanz scrolled her screen. "Unmarked. Fenced in. What the hell? He was so determined to keep San Lin in perpetual suffering that he buried them both far away from here...anonymously."

"Flashlights. Shovels. Heavier clothing." Baker stood. "Six tomorrow."

"It's all Masonic stuff. Albert was a Mason. I never

really thought much of it. There's something in the files saying he was a member of the Order of the Knights Templar. Masonic stuff is rife with mysticism. I'm thinking we *should* take the first ferry at 6 a.m."

Baker opened the flat file full of rocks and crystals. "Motherload! I'm going to pull together a protective grid to amplify anything in this room that's already protecting us."

"The least of the attacky possessions has been in this room. Go for it." Sanz began to make a list on her phone. "How far is your place, Baker?"

"Not far."

"All right. We'll leave early then."

"Yes. And I'll put on a pair of jeans and grab my flashlight."

She returned to her notetaking, glancing over her shoulder at Baker's crystal choices. "Talk to me, man."

"Obsidian. Black tourmaline. Selenite. Clear Quartz. Peridot. Real citrine. Uncut ruby. Wow, Sanz. He may have been an asshole, but he has some nice rocks."

"For protection, right?"

"Yeah. And grief. And success in business. Lots of things." He began creating a crystal grip by tracing a Metatron's Grid in the dust of a low credenza. "One good use for dust." He placed a quartz point in the center and upon each of the circle points radiating out from the center he placed a dark stone. Obsidian and black tourmaline.

"Let's get the windows covered."

"And use the UV light on the rest of the room first."

Tall enough to reach without much of a stretch, Baker replaced the velvet drapes. "Darkness falls."

Sanz pocketed her phone and retrieved the UV flashlight. "Doesn't need batteries. So, let's look." She started in the upper right-hand corner of the room and passed the purple beam over every book.

"Try the back of the pocket doors. Somewhere easy to write something."

She took a few steps closer to the door and illuminated the doors made of bell metal. "Good call, Baker." She said each letter as the UV light brought it to life. "48.6159° N, 123.1480° W."

"That's twice now we've discovered the location of Afterglow Vista."

"Why make it all so cryptic?" Sanz ran her fingertips over the illuminated numbers. "Christ, he was crazy."

"Did he like puzzles?"

She laughed. "Yes, actually. There are cupboards full of old puzzles."

"That's why. He didn't want to make it easy, but for some reason, he wanted someone to know the truth. I don't think the clown card is spirit writing. I think, in his dementia-ridden brain, he was seeking redemption."

"The egomaniac probably wants flowers on his grave on his birthday or something. Such a nudge." Sanz paused. "However, all his plans were laid out in his will. If he wanted pink roses on his grave, he would have said so."

"The missing ledger?"

"Maybe."

"Sanz, there's one place we haven't looked yet."

"Baker, there are a million places we haven't looked yet."

He laughed. "The toybox."

"I hate that thing."

"If the key fits...turn it."

Sanz had the golden key tucked into the thigh pocket on her yoga pants. "That would be too easy."

"Hey, all mysteries need to be solved in thirty minutes. Did you not watch cartoons?"

Sanz laughed. "All right. Let's go." As she slipped out the library she mumbled, "Freaking scary f-ing clown box."

Baker rested his hand on her shoulder. "It's all right."

A few moments later they stood on the opposite side of the plastic sheeting leading to the east wing. "I really hate that box. I admit it. I have coulrophobia. Fear of clowns."

"Who doesn't?" Baker spread the two plastic tarps to allow them to enter. "We got this, Sanz."

"Can't sleep. Clowns will eat me."

"I'll watch you tonight. Make sure you're safe."

Sanz leaned into him, sliding her head under his arm so that it ended up around her. "I think I need a little traditional teenager mating ritual to get the numbness in my feet and hands to end."

"Oh?" Baker swept her into his arms and put his mouth to hers.

She reached around his neck and held his head fast to hers. She melted into him and heard their kiss as a piece of classical music. It had the color of a golden sunset and felt like an eternal road stretched out before her. *He triggers my synesthesia in all the best ways.* She met his tongue as it breached her mouth. The kiss grew deeper. They held each other tighter. He raised on knee and slid it between her legs, his kilt climbing up his thigh. She pressed her nether regions against his leg. At long last a sense of panic overtook her and she broke the kiss. "We're being naughty, Baker."

"Yeah. I need a moment. I'm...I've got tumescence."
He turned away. Sanz grabbed his hips and turned him
around to face her.

"I won't take advantage of your arousal, but please...
can I see the rise in your kilt?"

"Men can't hide anything," Baker replied.

"Your poor sporran is floating above the fabric now,
isn't it?" She laughed and did her best not to reach up his
kilt.

"Something in this place—maybe it's you—makes
me aware that I have a man's body and a man's reactions
no matter how non-conforming my moral compass
may be."

"Tell you what, Baker...take a look at the clown
toybox. That will deflate anything."

He kissed her quickly and took the dozen or so steps
into the east wing to where the toybox lay, dusty,
chained, and grotesque. "Yep. Totally gone." He turned
the key in the lock as Sanz watched safely from behind,
holding her cell phone light for him.

"What's in it?"

The chains crashed to the floor. Dust flew up. Sanz
coughed. "I hate this wing."

"Nothing a good cleaning and airing wouldn't fix.
This could be an amazing place to hold homecoming,
don't you think?"

"What? The ballroom?" She paused. "Yes. It would be
awesome. If anyone would come to it."

"Everyone would come to it."

"When is it?" she asked.

"I'm not sure. May, maybe. Next month."

"Hmmm. If we survive this do we attend together in
matching corsages?"

"Biggest problem for me is that I'm feeling rather virile and a semi-formal dance makes me think of one thing."

"The proverbial roll in the hay? The backseat of Daddy's car? The perfunctory defloration of the virgins?"

Baker motioned for her to shine the light into the chest. "Yes."

"All right. I accept. We go out for Chinese then the dance—maybe even here, then we do the deed. Condom is a must. But I'm already on birth control pills to regulate my cycle."

Using both hands Baker lifted a tattered, ancient ledger book from the box. "Holy shit, Sanz."

She passed her flashlight over the cover. "Yep. Look at the date. 1965-1966."

"There's a lot of salt in the chest, too."

"Why of course there is." Sanz peeked over Baker and looked inside the chest. "Do you feel the change in the air?"

"Yes," he whispered.

"We let something loose, didn't we?"

Baker nodded. "I need to get out of here before Albert jumps me. Sanz...he wants to do bad things to you. He sees you as an extension of San Lin."

"Flee. Bring the ledger. She's never going to allow herself to be used again. I can feel she's got quite a bit of fight in her." *You go, Granny.*

Baker leaned in. "That's why she was murdered. He doesn't want the fight. He wants absolute submission."

"Lock up the toybox again, huh?"

Baker passed the ledger to her and reattached the chains and lock. They vibrated in his hands and he smelled rust and fear. "Let's get out of here."

Sanz led Baker downstairs and into the kitchen. "Food?"

He nodded as he replied to a text. "Mom is going to my aunt's house. She offered to drop off takeout for us. Jesus, it's hard to be a normal teenager when facing certain doom.

"Oooo...I get to meet your mother!"

"She's going to know. She has an innate sense of me and my relationships—and lack thereof. I would suggest waving from the front porch while I run to her powder blue EV."

"We haven't done anything untoward. Nothing kids our age don't engage in. Me...I figured I was a decade off before making out with someone. You...you didn't seem too interested in a relationship when first we conversed of such things."

"I didn't want one. Male or female, somewhere in-between or other—I didn't want one." He paused and looked hard at Sanz. "I do now."

She nodded. "So do I." She held out her right-hand pinky finger. "Homecoming night?"

He linked his pinky with hers. "Homecoming night."

"You going to that homecoming dance?" It was Bergie.

"Yeah, Ma. We were thinking of going together for shits and giggles." Sanz leaned against the counter trying to look incredibly casual.

"That's lovely, dear. Look...I'm going to go lay down for a while. I swear the energies in this house are giving me a headache. Be good, kids."

"Yes, ma'am," Baker replied. The moment Bergie was out of sight, Baker moved behind Sanz and pressed her to the kitchen counter. He kissed the side of her throat. His strong arms moved around her waist. His fingertips darted inside the waistband of her yoga pants. When she moaned, he reached farther inside to caress her hips and buttocks. Boldly, he moved his right hand over her mons, atop her panties. His middle finger slid over her clit. He didn't stop. She responded to his touch by placing her hand atop his over her nether regions. He rubbed her over her panties for a bit, then slid under them. *She's wet.* He inserted two fingers into her and used his thumb to continue stroking her clitoris. He felt her entire body quake and shatter and pressed his hardness into her backside as he brought her to orgasm.

Sanz took a deep breath, but didn't move away. She turned in his arms and reached up his kilt. She pulled the slit of his black boxer briefs aside and felt his member. "Is tonight the homecoming?"

He planted his lips against hers as Sanz took control of the situation. Took control of his penis. She stroked him. "Too dry," she whispered. She turned slightly and took a nob of butter into her hand and returned to him. Slicked by the organic grass-fed fat, she stroked him to orgasm. It didn't take long.

He rested against her. "Christ, Sanz."

"Prayerfully spoken."

"I need to clean up. I kind of spilled on my shorts."

"I think this is like Chinese food. Will we want more in an hour?" She rinsed her hands in the sink.

Baker wet a kitchen towel and wiped his ardor away, depositing the cloth in the washer.

They returned to the library with the heavy ledger in tow.

Sanz plopped down onto the sofa. "Well, that was unexpected and just...perfect."

"I very much want to make it to the dance to make love. But I don't think we'll make it. The sight of you makes me hard. Your touch sends me through the roof. I've never experienced this before."

"Likewise. I've fooled around a little. You know...hand jobs." She looked up at him through her mascara-blackened eyelashes. "Blow jobs."

"Yeah. And I've performed cunnilingus and actually a blow job—but never went all the way."

"I'm on the pill, man."

"Is this us or is it the energy of this place? The men used to take satisfaction in such sick ways and the girls...all I feel from them is terror." He looked at his phone. "Mom's here. Fuck. I need to be calm before my mother when my heart is racing and I just came. This feels like it should be more secret than beating off in my room. But there's really no reason for us to be a secret, is there?"

Sanz followed Baker out the front door and waved sweetly at his mom. "No reason at all. My mother would be relieved to know I'm acting *normal*."

He retrieved the bag of Chinese food and dashed up the steps to the porch. "Mom says hey."

"Hey to Mom."

"Great. Another pair of briefs. Clean t-shirt, my flannel jacket. Pajama bottoms...and damn...she packed my eyeliner...and a toothbrush and condom. I didn't tell her we're leaving for San Juan in the morning. But thanks, Mom."

"Moms know best."

"She's been hopeful for a while."

"Let's look at the ledger before we get carried away again," Sanz suggested.

"By ourselves or the spirits haunting this place. I agree."

"You make my nipples hard, Baker."

He coughed. "You're welcome."

They set the ledger across their laps as they ate, and carefully flipped through the pages. The old, yellowed, brittle paper cracked under their touch.

"Accounting shit. Always accounting. How many bushels of salt. How many cases of whiskey." Sanz turned a page and stopped. "Looks at this."

"It's a sketch. A fence. Wrought iron."

"On the trail to Afterglow Vista there are a handful of graves—unmarked but fenced off. I saw it online. He must be buried in one of those. Which means San Lin is buried in one of those."

"Tomorrow, we put her to rest." Baker clinked Sanz's can of soda as if toasting.

"Tomorrow."

"Egg roll?" Baker asked.

"Yes, please."

They ate the four-item combo meals provided by Baker's mother in the half-light and sat quietly, holding hands.

"What a day, huh?" Sanz joked.

"Yes. It's been one for the books. The energy in this room is quiet. I think the crystal grid may be helping. That and all the salt."

"Good. I don't think I can take another smack-down from Albert."

"I'm really sorry, Sanz. I've never channeled so physi- cally and vehemently before. With all that I am, believe me, that wasn't me."

"I know. Do you want to see the chapel? Or walk to the lighthouse? Get out of here for a bit?"

"Both."

"Drop that 3-pack of Trojans into your sporran. I'm not saying I won't be able to keep my hands off you, but there's always that chance."

"We can wait a month. Can we wait a month?"

Sanz laughed. "I've waited a long time to feel this way. I've never been in heat before. And it cracks me up that amidst all the stuff that's happened to us today, that I still want to..." she paused thoughtfully, forming the words. She could see them before her eyes as she spoke them. Fireworks. "Do unspeakable things to you."

"It might be kind of fun not to go all the way. Think of the frustration. Glorious." Baker turned and kissed her. "Sweet torture."

"All right. All right. Let's take the rest of this feast to the lighthouse, huh? I walked there a few days ago. I can't believe it's left open."

"Beacon Shores is very trusting."

"How long has it been maintained, but unused?"

"The 1970's sometime. And like this house...someone put it into perpetual care."

"Is it a hangout place? Drug den?"

"No. No graffiti either. Did you go all the way to the top?"

They walked out the front of the manor and began the trek to the lighthouse—which could be seen on the jetty not too far away. "I did not. I peeked inside and since I'm here for the duration, figured I'd find someone nice to go with me."

Baker laughed. "I'm nice."

"Yes. Yes, you are." Sanz took his hand. "All right Beacon Shores…look at this! Young persons in heat!"

"We are that. But I think we are more than that, too."

"Most certainly. No one else has been playing ping-pong possession with me."

"Yeah. I'm really done with that." Baker stopped. "Let's get my truck on the way. I'll grab a pair of jeans, too. That's the only thing Mom didn't pack."

"Where's your house?"

"If you look directly at the lighthouse, look right to the end of the road, then count four houses down from the gas station. It's light blue with black trim."

"I see it."

"Let's go. Mom isn't home. Dad works late."

CHAPTER EIGHT

The walk to Baker's house was done in silence with only stolen glances between them. The late afternoon sun was warm and the ever-present view of the bay, calming. Beacon Shores had bike trails and foot paths everywhere. Sanz had thought Portland was the hub of liberal nature lovers—but no. Here, on the edge of the United States close to the Canadian border, was a nest of relaxation. Beacon Shores. With its horrific history now charmed into submission by free WIFI, recreation areas and small-town atmosphere, it was lovely. Any roil in her gut was forced into submission. *Everything is going to be okay. I'm not a freaking Pollyanna, but I just know it. Is this the inherited psychic ability from great to the fourth power granny?* She recognized that Baker caused her more fluctuations of mind and body than did the hauntings. *Something is wrong there. Apparently, nothing can stop teenaged lust.*

Baker's house was a standard three-bedroom two-bath ranch style. Except for the crystal grids on the coffee table, kitchen counter, hallway bathroom shelf and then there was Baker's room. Bright yellow.

"Suffer from depression, Baker? Hoping that sunshine yellow will keep you off lithium?"

"Kind of. This brilliant shade of yellow helps me sleep. I know that's odd, but then so am I." He stripped off his kilt and stood before her in his black boxer briefs. And then he grabbed a clean pair and almost shyly stepped into his adjoining bathroom to change out of the sedate black briefs that were the only evidence of their naughtiness.

Sanz frowned. *Well, damn. I'm not that shy. Guess he's waiting for the wedding night to show me the goods.* She laughed aloud, and Baker stepped out with a confused look on his face.

She recovered well. *Smart ass remark needs to be inserted here.* "You in your briefs against the wall gives off honeybee vibes." *Oh, my God...he has incredible thigh muscles. Why am I going through this? I am highly intelligent and will someday take over NASA and the space program. I shouldn't be so distracted by a boy. A beautiful, almost nineteen-year-old boy with fabulous muscles who diddled me in my kitchen. And I let him. I'm losing my grip on reality.*

He slipped into an old pair of Levi's with ripped knees and instead of his Doc Martens, put on Chucks. "Close your mouth, Sanz. I'm not that impressive."

"Oh, crap. Am I drooling?"

"Let's go." He took her by the upper arm and guided her out of his room and into the garage.

"Your parents have a three-car finished garage and the only thing in here is your truck and a ton of boxes."

"Mom doesn't throw anything away. She stores things for later use. It's a problem. She has all my baby clothes sealed in a box that is properly labeled and stacked in chronological order."

"And I thought my mom has issues. Oh wait...in my family it's hereditary. I mean...*Albert*, yanno?"

He opened the truck door for her. She climbed in and before she realized the vehicle did not have shoulder harnesses—only a lap belt—they were off.

"You've done some work in here. I smell new fabric."

"Yep. I restored the interior. It was a rat's nest before I bought it. Sat in a barn for forty years."

Short drive. No stoplights. One sign. The jetty was fully paved and the lighthouse graced its end. They took their bag of food and entered the beacon of Beacon Shores through that trusting unlocked door and began the climb to the top.

"It's not needed any longer to guide coal export ships, but the light will come on during the holidays."

"Albie built this, too, didn't he?"

Baker nodded. "Yes. But it's no longer in the family. It's fully owned by the Beacon Historical Society. I kind of figure that I'll end up running BHS later in life. I will add ghost tours to the brochure, however."

"Thank goodness. I like this place. It is for me, truly a 'light' house of a lighthouse. I do not feel a bit of haunting here and nothing is setting off my synesthesia —except you from time to time."

"Yeah? Do my steps sound like musical notes or something?"

"When you hold me, I can literally taste your heartbeat and your aura is huge. Radiant."

He turned on the spiral stairs and swept her into his arms and up against the railing. "You mean hold you like this?"

She nodded. "Your heartbeat tastes like cotton candy." Sanz paused for a moment and closed her eyes. "And the rest of your body is sheet music. I hear music from your upper arms and thighs. And other places."

"My kiss?" He put his mouth to hers and whispered, "What does my kiss sing to you?"

"Bohemian Rhapsody."

"And my fingers?" He ran his fingertips over her breasts.

"Frank Sinatra."

"Really? I like being *that* smooth."

They embraced carefully. It was clear that one wrong step would send them spiraling down the stairs.

"Come on, Sanz. Let's get to the top. The view is insane."

So am I. "Yes. Let's."

There was little to say as they ate. The 360-degree view was, indeed, breathtaking. "The house doesn't look so ominous from up here. And I'm not going to fret over lack of conversation here. That view says it all. And we're eating." She paused. "We haven't run out of conversation, have we?"

"How does it smell?" Baker asked. "The house."

"I may see a fine old Victorian-style mansion out the north window, but it smells like wet dog."

"Sweet."

They laughed.

Sanz had her phone on vibrate. "Oh, dear. Text from Ma."

I saw you holding hands with Baker.

Sanz replied quickly.

"Yes. We are a thing now. It's all right."

I thought he was gay.

He's demi. I really like him. He makes me feel safe.

All right. Is he still spending the night? Please don't have loud, athletic sex in the library.

We're not there yet, Ma.

Something is stirred up in the house. That poltergeist activity has increased, fyi.

Yeah?

"Mom says the poltergeist is acting up."

"No doubt. We'll be back there soon. Let's finish our fried rice."

We're eating at the lighthouse. Be home soon.

"She should go stay in the library. Goliath is warded." Baker squeezed her upper arm supportively.

"She has been bothered before. Nothing serious. But I don't really want my mother sleeping in the library with us tonight, you know?"

"To protect your mother from ghostly advances, you don't want her with us?"

"Can we make a protective grid in her bedroom? And no, I don't want my mother watching us tonight."

"It's not homecoming. We won't be doing the deed."

"She already covered that. She saw us holding hands out her bedroom window."

"I'm proud to have public displays of affection with you, Sanz."

"I'm glad. Because keeping my hands off you is going to be difficult. You are heretofore in my safety zone, Baker."

"I accept."

Sanz wasn't sure how she got there, but Baker's smooth moves had her on the concrete floor with him nearly fully atop her a moment later. Like kids rolling around in the backseat of Daddy's car...they melted into each other and became a cacophony of mouths and hands and a bit of grinding and lots of moaning. She wrapped her legs around his and held him fast. He moved atop her as if they were having intercourse. Each thrust ushered forth a huge blast of music in her mind until an entire symphony filled her. She raised her hips to meet his jeans-clad advances. She reached between them and felt the rise in his pants. He lifted her shirt and kissed her bosom over her bra.

"Is this safe sex?" she giggled as she rolled him and took a superior position.

"I may have to throw out these jeans, but yes."

"Well, we wouldn't want to soil a perfectly good pair of Levis now, would we?" She fumbled with his button fly. "I hate all these buttons."

"Consider it a modern-day chastity belt. Leave them on. We can rub against each other pleasurably and still wear our virgin rings."

"No...you need to be released from the confines of your breeches, sir. Or it will look like you wet yourself."

"I've got a pair of work pants in the truck. Carhartt.

Paint-stained, but they will be fine. I do odd jobs from time to time around here."

Sanz laughed and moved atop him as if they were in full coitus. *I want to achieve orgasm here or I will be flailing in a few minutes. Rub a dub dub.*

Baker held her hips and trust into her nether regions, so sedately covered by panties and black yoga pants.

Climax was simultaneous. Magnificent. Wet, hot and smelled like a sulfuric geyser in the wilds of Iceland surrounded by purple lupins and happy lambs, tails wagging at mother's milk.

"Oh, dear gods." She rolled off and waited for her heart to quit beating so fast. "Never have I experienced something so rich."

Baker patted his damp crotch area. "Yeah. Fuck me."

"Umm...I think I just did."

"I told you not going all the way would be satisfying."

"For now." She leaned forward and kissed him, then stood. "All right, let's pack up and head home. Mother must be atop a chair shrieking by now."

"This isn't all I want from you. I just need you to know that."

"Well, Baker...this doesn't seem to be interfering with our plan to pull the rubber mask off the bad guy—and in fact, it's helping me stay focused if you can believe that. The release is great."

He laughed. "Yes, well...I released all over myself. It's far easier to splooge cleanly when wearing a kilt. Are you...all right?"

"The resultant effects of my climax are hidden inside serene yet stylish black panties and yoga pants. I'm fine. No worse for the wear."

They breezed down the spiral staircase as the sun set

all around them. Brilliant oranges and pinks filled the sky and the moon rose red and ominous. They stood at the edge of the jetty for a few moments to admire the sky of eventide. A slight breeze kicked up gentle, rolling white-caps and in the distance a buoy chimed in warning of shallows.

"Sunset and moonrise have never looked more beautiful. It sounds like apples falling from a tree and tastes like tacos."

Baker cracked up. "I wish I could taste the sky that way. Tacos? Really?"

Sanz nodded. She climbed into the cab while Baker fished out his work pants and changed. Both his fresh black briefs and jeans went behind the bench seat.

"All right, Sanz...let's go rest up before we solve the mystery."

"And rob a grave after finding it."

"It's nice to commit a sacrilegious crime with you, girl."

Sanz continued. "Then transport stolen items on a state vessel and rebury them in a grave not lined by lead, as is the custom."

"This will make a great book. Are you taking notes?" Baker asked. He rested a hand on her leg.

"I forget nothing. *A Fine Collection of Sins*, or *What Albert Did Under the Witch's Cap*."

"We can work on the title later."

———

Baker parked on the conservatory side and they entered through the kitchen. "Everyone in Beacon is now going to know I'm staying the night."

"Does anyone care?"

Baker shrugged. "Because it's my truck and the Whittie house...maybe. I'll share any interesting texts I get with you. My friends might message me about it. I don't know. As you have previously noticed, nothing happens here and anything new from the haunted mansion is bound to get a few comments."

"I can live with that. I've never really cared what others say or think. I figure I'm smarter and even with my so-called handicap, am still more well-adjusted." Sanz stopped him in the grand foyer. "Gotta tell ya...the omnipresent feeling of not being alone is riding shotgun."

"Yeah. We're back and they know it."

Baker and Sanz proceeded to set up crystal grids around the entire house.

"It's okay, Ma. Really. I think it will help."

Her mother said nothing but watched with interest. Especially when Baker set up a grid atop the evil clown toybox. Mother's room, kitchen, east wing, conservatory. The room under the witch's cap. Sanz didn't want to go up there. "Hey, dude...I trust you. Do what you will."

Baker laughed and climbed the narrow steps with a baggie full of crystals, paper and sharpie. Sanz watched him intently. His work pants hung low on his waist and the top of his butt showed. She sighed. *I am lost to teenage sexual urges. And here I thought my eighteenth year would be far less interesting.*

"You like him, huh?"

"Yes, Mom. I like him."

"Is he a witch?"

"I think so, yes. When we have more time I'll tell you about the punches to the gut he receives from this place."

Bergie nodded. "Yes. The paperwork did not say the

house is haunted. And it is. I hope his little crystals help." She held out her arm. "I've got bruises. I want to call one of those shows that covers poltergeist activity."

Sanz touched her mother's bruised arm. "It will help, Ma."

Bergie patted Sanz on the shoulder as she walked away and without looking back, said softly, "Use protection."

"Yes, Ma."

Sanz met Baker at the base of the stair to the turret. "Hi. Am I about to kiss Baker, San Lin, or Albert?"

"I wasn't attacked. The grids are holding. So, kiss me. Baker. I promise to kiss you back."

"I never thought I would ever feel this...horny. Satisfied. Terrified with gut-wrenching fear of doom. Fill in the blank." Sanz kissed him.

"I wasn't looking for a relationship. But something deep inside me told me to walk up the jetty to meet the new girl. So glad I did."

"We might have a quiet night, huh? Every crystal in Albie's collection is now being utilized to neutralize the restless spirits of this place."

"Flat file is emptied of both protective and stones of amplification."

"Mom wants us to use protection."

Baker chuckled. "Tell Mom we don't have enough crystals for anything else."

CHAPTER NINE

Books scattered around them, the ominous ledger open, a ferry schedule unfolded and the more interesting of the artifacts in Goliath explored, they settled onto a throw rug with pillows and blankets. Baker had donned his pajama bottoms and Sanz a cotton nightgown.

"I'm almost afraid to sleep," she said.

"There's a salt ring around us, babe. And outside that ring, more salt. And crystal grids. We are doing what San Lin wants us to do. Removing her from eternal torment. She won't show up."

"We are also doing that which Albert does not want."

Baker showed her the palm of his right hand. He'd used the sharpie to mark himself with the same protective runes carved into the pocket doors. "Just in case." He kissed her. "Good night, Sanz. We need to get up and out around 5 a.m. That's way early."

Sanz snuggled up against him and rested her head on his chest. "May we sleep in safety."

———

Her first ferry ride proved uneventful. Sanz insisted on standing at the bow to feel the salt spray and wind.

"You are going to be cold and wet," Baker said as he tried to usher her back to his truck.

"Not much to a ferry ride, huh? The boat chugs away and I haven't seen a whale. Total bummer."

"We can take a whale-watching tour. Come back to the truck and drink your coffee before it's as cold as your hands are."

"Yes, dear."

The excursion took thirty minutes. The first two stops were quick. Weekday morning, apparently most were exiting the islands instead of returning to them. The ferry docked in Friday Harbor with a small thud and the handful of vehicles disembarked.

Baker pulled out an old map of San Juan Island from the glove box. "Where's Afterglow Vista?"

"Other side of the island. Roche Harbor."

"I've been here a dozen times and never knew about the rich man's mausoleum on a hill. We went to American Camp and English Camp on field trips in middle school. And my parents and I stayed at a B&B for a weekend retreat once."

"Retreat from what?"

"I don't know. I played video games the entire weekend while my parents communed. Food was good."

"Anyplace around here to get a burger?" Sanz asked.

"Yeah. We can catch something at Roche Harbor, I think. It's a boating community. Never been there—but that's about to change."

"The instructions online said we need to drive up a

"private access only" road next to the entrance to Roche Harbor, turn right onto a dirt road and park. Then it's all uphill. We should pass the fenced in graves on our way to Afterglow Vista. There are some travel blogs that speak highly of this little trip."

"They weren't looking for a specific grave. To dig up. And bust open. And separate bones."

"This is true. We'll be the first. Should I record our clandestine behavior for our book?"

"Definitely." Baker observed the speed limit while Sanz marveled at the organic honey, milk, produce, and egg signs along the route. The drive took twenty minutes.

He turned up the only "private access road" and drove to the first dirt roadway, proceeded forward then parked once they spotted a rather well-worn trail.

"All right. Shovels. Gloves. Bags."

"Don't forget candles, incense, protective crystals and intestinal fortitude." Sanz giggled.

"It's all in my knapsack. Let's go."

She opened the passenger door and met Baker at the trailhead. "A kiss for luck?"

He kissed her quickly then started up the trail. Within a half mile, the first of the gravestones appeared on the slope.

"Three fenced-in graves. All wooden pickets except that one," Sanz pointed to the odd ball fence. "Which is metal."

"And the marker is toppled. Well...shall we begin there? It's also the only marker without a name. Although I don't read Japanese and the other markers are in Hiragana, which I do recognize."

"Can you get all psychic on the grave and see if it's the

right one before we commit a felony?" Sanz slipped on the work gloves.

"It's the right one. I'm surprised the earth hasn't swallowed us up or anything." He walked to the wrought iron fence and dropped a chunk of clear quartz on each side. "She's here, Sanz."

"Hello, Great Granny. We're going to rescue you now."

"She knows."

Using collapsible shovels from Baker's garage they jumped the fence and began digging. "It's pretty damned early for others to be hiking right now. We should be unobserved. I hope we don't get arrested. Mother would shit."

"We're doing God's work. The only thing that can stop us is Albert."

Sanz looked up from her pile of dirt. "Think he'll try?" She tried to do that math in her head. Burial in 1966 of a fresh corpse plus hundred-year-old bones. *What is the degradation rate? How gnarly is this going to be?* "I'm going into aerospace engineering after community college. Trying to do the math on this is a brain boggle. I don't recall the decomp rate for bodies circa 1966 burials. I could text Ma, but she'd ask why."

"I'm glad you have a boyfriend now, Sanz. You need more to worry about besides the decomp rate of 1966 corpses." His shovel hit wood. "Woah. Not too far down. Let's dig this out."

They began clearing the dirt and found a wooden box. Not a coffin. Warily they dug out the plain brown box. "He's not in a coffin. This is a cremation box," Sanz said. "I mean...this is kind of my mom's forte."

Baker reached into the three-foot hole and pulled

out the box. "It's pretty solid. And sealed." He hit it with the edge of his shovel and the top caved in. "All righty then. A decrepit bag of cremains and—" he pushed the bag over with his shovel. "Bones. Her bones."

"She said she was intertwined with him."

Baker stood up straight and then fell back against the fence. His face grew ashen and eyes rolled back. "Do not leave me here!"

"Baker?" *God damn it. It's happening again.*

"Granddaughter...remove my ashes from his and rebury my bones with my ancestors."

Oh, he doesn't look good. "Are you hurting Baker?"

"Remove my ashes from his and rebury my bones."

"I think you need to let him go. He looks as though he's going to convulse."

Baker shook off the heaviness of spirit possession. "Please...leave me now." It was more an order than a request. "I can't take any more of this." He took a couple of deep breaths and regained composure. Freed of the spirit, he looked at his hand. "Screw these runes. Didn't help. Nor did the crystals."

"I think she's in a separate bag inside his. Buried *in* his. What a sick fuck. Torturing her in life and in death."

Baker pulled himself to his feet and took a deep breath. He slipped on his work gloves and using his pen knife, slit open the cremains. He then took a twig and stirred the ashes. "This is so gross."

"There. There! A ratty cloth bag." Sanz clapped her hands with giddiness. "I've seen lots of cremains. I'm not affected by them. Can you lift out the cloth sack?"

"I got it." He lifted a loosely knotted bag from the ashes of Albert Whitmore and set it aside. With his gloved hand he removed the bones. "Small bones. Fingers? Toes?"

"Doesn't matter. Just get all of them." Sanz picked up the box and dropped it back into the grave and frantically began shoveling dirt. "I need to get this done. I have a pressing need to get to Afterglow Vista. *She* wants to visit there. Now that we've separated the wheat from the chaff, I'm sure things should improve. Although I feel like I've been punched in the stomach."

Baker patted down the dirt atop the plot and repositioned the headstone. "Have you ever been punched?"

"Only by Albert."

"I've taken my share of blows boxing and wrestling. I want you to know that a psychic punch is way worse. You can feel the energy to your bones."

The grave looked disturbed. Not much could be done about changing freshly tilled earth to moss-covered *old*. "Someone is going to know." Sanz picked up the crystals from around the wrought iron fence.

"There are no cameras and most people are still in bed having coffee and looking at TikTok videos. We'll be fine. Let's keep climbing. I want to take this non-descript black trash bag with me to Afterglow. Not sure why I shouldn't just lock it in the truck, but I'm going to go with my gut." Baker slung the bag over his shoulder like Santa with his toys.

"Agreed. Let's take the shovels, too. Just in case. I know that the McMillans' cremains are all interred in marble chairs. But just in case we need to dig."

"Dates with you are so much fun, Sanz. I've never taken shovels on an outing to dig up a grave before. Promise me we'll always have fun." Baker chuckled at his own joke.

"We'll figure something out. Let's trek."

Afterglow Vista came into view after a few minutes up the trail.

Sanz stopped to read the plaque aloud.

"The structure is approached by two sets of stairs, representing the steps within the Masonic Order. The stairs on the east side of the mausoleum stand for the spiritual life of man. The winding in the path symbolizes that the future cannot be seen. The stairs were built in sets of three, five and seven. This represents the three stages of life (youth, manhood, age), the five orders of architecture Tuscan, Doric, Iconic, Corinthian, Composite), the five senses, and the seven liberal arts and sciences (grammar, rhetoric, logic, arithmetic, geometry, music, astronomy).

The columns were created to be the same size as those in King Solomon's temple. The broken column represents the broken column of life-that man dies before his work is completed."

She paused and interjected, "That's depressing." She continued reading

"The center of the mausoleum boasts the round table of limestone and concrete surrounded by six stone and concrete chairs. The chair bases are crypts for the ashes of the family, while the whole represents their reunion after death. The construction of the mausoleum began in 1930 and was completed to its present state by the spring of 1936 at a cost of approximately $30,000. McMillin had planned to erect a bronze dome with the

Maltese cross atop the edifice. He had ordered the dome, but his son, Paul, cancelled the order, as the company did not have the $20,000 it would cost."

"That is wicked smart."

"It's said that on that right-hand side stairway that represents that the path cannot be seen, folks been ghost-pushed."

"They ain't got nothing on what we've experienced."

Baker and Sanz walked up to the huge limestone table and began reading the chairbacks. "Knights of the Templar. Masonic stuff. Albie was also a Knight Templar," she said. "This place is insane."

Sanz walked to the edge of the stairs and pathway on the right side of the monument. "Oh, Baker. There is something here. I can taste it. Tingles in the air. It's like pop rocks."

"I'm getting goosebumps. Let's jet, huh? I don't think San Lin wants to be reburied here."

"Agreed. It's too far from her family. We should deposit her ashes and bones in the place where her daughters are buried."

"Where the hell is that?" Baker asked.

"We don't have an official family cemetery on grounds, but I bet those little girl babies who died in the mines—or were drowned with her—have a burial plot nearby the house."

"More reading of the ledgers to be done?"

"Maybe. But I think she can lead us to where she'd like to be." Sanz paused. "I need to sit down. Baker...she's here."

Baker helped Sanz to one of the stone chairs filled with the ashes of a McMillan child. "I see it, babe."

Before them, hovering in the broken column was a wisp of a girl. Dark hair and eyes. Thin, but belly distended by pregnancy. Sad, but radiating determination.

Baker spoke as Sanz was too overwrought to even lift her head. "San Lin."

"Lover of my granddaughter."

Baker nodded. "What can we do to help you?"

"I need to tell you my story."

Sanz pulled herself upright. "Please," she replied to the apparition.

To be continued in
A Fine Collection of Sins Book Two: Afterglow

ABOUT THE AUTHOR

Goshen Hexx is enjoying reliving her high school and early college days by writing new adult romances. A good girl who never caused any problems or fooled around until she was older finds that writing such amazing and satisfying burgeoning romances between young people is incredibly rewarding. Goshen has, on the other hand, had many experiences with the supernatural and paranormal because her mother was a spiritualist minister, and she is an accomplished tarot and Rune reader.